Dear Reader,

Hormones? If Jenny wants me to believe that's all it was, she's got another thing coming. That kiss left her trembling—I could feel her ragged breath against my cheek, her heart pounding.... If it was just hormones, why did she run away? Why did she stay away so long?

Now, after five years without a word, she's back in Iowa, acting like she's never been gone, like nothing ever happened between us. But I don't believe her act. She knows as well as I do that fight it as she might, it's just a matter of time before she's back in my arms.

Dane Sutherland

LEIGH MICHAELS

Leigh Michaels is the author of more than seventy contemporary romances for Harlequin Books. More than twenty-seven million copies of her books have been printed worldwide. Six of her books have been finalists for Best Traditional Romance novel in the RITA® Award contest sponsored by Romance Writers of America. Leigh was also the 2003 recipient of the Johnson Brigham Plaque, awarded every two to three years by the Iowa Library Association to "the Iowa author for the most outstanding contribution to literature."

She is the author of *Writing the Romance Novel*, a how-to guide for romance writers, in addition to a series of audio tapes on writing and the romance genre. She teaches an annual seminar on the romance novel at the University of Iowa and has written articles for *Writer's Digest* and *The Writer*.

A native Iowan, she received a bachelor of arts in journalism from Drake University in Des Moines, Iowa.

Leigh
Michaels

Kiss Yesterday
Goodbye

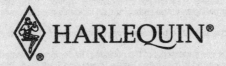

TORONTO • NEW YORK • LONDON
AMSTERDAM • PARIS • SYDNEY • HAMBURG
STOCKHOLM • ATHENS • TOKYO • MILAN • MADRID
PRAGUE • WARSAW • BUDAPEST • AUCKLAND

ISBN 0-373-36018-5

KISS YESTERDAY GOODBYE

Copyright © 1984 by Leigh Michaels

Published Harlequin Enterprises, Ltd. 1984, 1993

Printed in U.S.A.

CHAPTER ONE

GREY CLOUDS scudded across the low sky, promising to bring snow before morning. But Jenny Ashley paid no attention to the threatening clouds, or to the cold that bit through her ski jacket, as she walked along the path beside the deep lagoon. Her head was bent and her hands were jammed in the pockets of the down jacket.

She kicked a stone off the snowy path and watched it splash into the water, the ripples widening out to the bank. A mallard duck, startled by her passing, flew from under a bush and splashed awkwardly into the water.

Jenny pulled the knit stocking cap down tighter around her ears and blew on her mittened hands. Watching the ducks was not an ideal pastime for a December day, but it was better than sitting in that tiny waiting room up at the hospital, waiting for the next time her father could have a visitor. And after an eight-hour drive, sitting any more was the last thing she wanted to do.

It frightened her, that her father was so ill that he was only allowed visitors once an hour. And the nurses had refused to make an exception, even if Jenny had just got into town.

She had argued with them, but the head nurse of the intensive care unit had been adamant. 'I'm sorry, Miss Ashley,' she had said, not sounding sorry for an instant. 'The rules are made for the good of the patient. Your mother just came out half an hour ago and went home for a rest.'

'I believe you mean my stepmother,' Jenny had corrected coolly.

'I mean Mrs Ashley,' the nurse said, not to be proved incorrect. 'You may go in half an hour from now. Not until then.'

Jenny kicked another stone off the path and looked at her watch. She wished she had asked the nurse which army she had been trained in. 'Probably Mussolini's,' she murmured. But at least being out in the fresh air was better than sitting in that stuffy waiting room.

'Would you like a slice of bread?'

The suddenness of the question startled Jenny, for she hadn't realised anyone else was nearby. She spun around to face the young man who had spoken.

He was hatless, with a stray fleck of snow in his wavy blond hair. He held out a plastic bread wrapper. 'To feed the ducks,' he explained unnecessarily. His gaze openly admired her dark brown eyes, framed in lashes so thick and dark they looked sooty, and the creamy complexion. 'Would you like to feed them?' he asked.

He tore a slice of bread in half and tossed it into the water, watching as two male mallards snapped at it, their green heads and ringed necks brilliant against the grey water.

Jenny reached into the wrapper. 'Thank you. I haven't fed the ducks in years,' she said thoughtfully, almost to herself, remembering those Sunday afternoons of her childhood which had nearly always included her father, a bag of day-old bread from the bakery, and the ducks. It was a habit in Twin Rivers to feed the ducks year round, and the growing flock of wild birds reflected it. She tore the slice of bread into small pieces and flung it into the water.

'It won't be long before the lagoon starts to freeze over,' the young man said. 'I really feel sorry for them then.'

'They wouldn't have it any other way,' Jenny mused. 'But I agree with you. If they stop paddling, it freezes right in around them. I've felt that way sometimes—as though if I stopped paddling for an instant, I'd freeze solid!' She looked up and smiled. 'Sorry, I'm not usually such a philosopher.'

'I don't mind. You're new around here, aren't you?'

'No. But I haven't been back to Twin Rivers in years.' She noted, quite calmly, that she had not said, 'I haven't been home in years.' It had ceased to be home five years ago when she had that last flaming quarrel with her father.

She glanced at her watch. What if, right now, up

in the hospital, he was dying? Stop it, Jenny, she told herself. People don't always die of heart attacks these days. He's past the first two days; that's the hardest.

'Are you staying long?'

'Probably just a few days.' She'd stay until her father was out of danger, if he wanted to see her at all. She wouldn't be surprised if he wouldn't let her come in. They had not parted on good terms five years ago, and there had been plenty of opportunity for others to convince him that he should forget he'd ever had a daughter.

'You picked a rotten season to be a tourist in Iowa.'

Jenny smiled unwillingly. 'Oh, I don't know. I'll take winter any day. I'm at my best when it's cold outside.'

'If that's true, you should consider staying the winter. It's colder here than any place else I've ever been, especially along in February when the outdoor thermometers start coming inside to get thawed out.'

'You're not a native, are you? I don't remember you.'

'My name is Steve Whitman.' He held out a large hand. 'I'm from Arizona originally, and I plan to go back. I'm assistant manager over at Twin Rivers Bakeries.' He misinterpreted her startled look. 'It's one of the biggest industries here—except for the university, that is. Twin Rivers, the cookie capital of the world.'

'I know bread and cookies are big business. I didn't know the company had been sold.'

'It hasn't; Dick Ashley still controls it down to the last mixing bowl. But when he brought in the new manager, they decided it should have a bigger name than just the Ashley Bakeries.'

Jenny said between clenched teeth, 'And tell me—does this new manager just happen to be named Dane Sutherland?'

'Yes. Do you know Dane?'

'I certainly do. He's been plotting to take over the Ashleys for the last ten years…'

The sentence was broken off in the middle as something red and furry slammed into the small of Jenny's back, catapulting her almost to the edge of the bank.

Steve's face was white as he bent over her. 'Are you all right? Can you get up?'

Jenny shook her head to clear it. 'What hit me?'

'That stupid dog. Get off her, you mutt!' He grabbed at the Irish setter's collar to haul him away. 'It's lucky he wasn't travelling any faster or you'd have had a swim.'

'Not exactly the weather for it,' Jenny murmured, still shaken.

Steve turned to the dark-haired man who followed the dog. 'I've told you before that if I ever see that dog roaming loose, I'll shoot him,' he threatened. 'He almost pushed the lady into the lagoon!'

'Steve, you know Finnegan wouldn't purposely hurt anybody. Any harm done?' The man brushed Steve aside and dropped to one knee beside Jenny.

The dog, abruptly realising he had done wrong, put his sorrowful nose on her knee, his plumed tail dropping dispiritedly.

Jenny looked up, startled. Her enormous brown eyes met the grey ones of the man kneeling beside her, who rocked back on his heels. 'Well, hello, Red,' he said calmly. 'I should have known it would be you in the middle of the storm.'

'That's right, put all the blame on me!' she snapped. 'If that isn't just like you, Dane Sutherland! I didn't exactly tell the dog to jump on me.'

'What a comfort. We're taking up exactly where we left off. Don't you want to add any choice remarks about my character and animal instincts as you did last time?'

Jenny struggled to her feet and brushed the snow off the seat of her jeans. 'Not just at present. But I'd like to say a few words about that damned dog of yours!—I assume he is yours?'

'The doubtful honour is all mine. Finnegan has very little brain—but he's a good listener when he isn't chasing rabbits or knocking people down.' The setter looked up at the peaceable note in his master's voice. His tail thumped against Jenny's knee a couple of times.

'Don't think I'm going to applaud you!' she told the dog fiercely.

'See what I mean? He's a real four-footed imbecile. He thinks you're the type who'll be kind to animals and other creatures in need of concern.'

'Do you have to practise being nasty or does it come naturally?' Jenny asked. 'How I have missed your so-called charms.'

His eyes brightened. 'Have you really, Red?' he asked, his voice suddenly intimately husky. 'Is that an invitation?'

'Don't call me Red!'

'Why? Have you started dyeing your hair?' Dane's hand shot out and plucked the stocking cap from her head. He pushed it into his pocket and ran a rough hand down the masses of red-gold hair that had tumbled from under the cap, falling past her shoulders. 'If that isn't red, what do you call it? Have you two met, by the way? Jenny Ashley—Steve Whitman. And you're wrong about one thing, Steve; let me warn you right now. Whatever else Red is, she is not a lady.'

Steve had been staring at Jenny's shining hair as she shook it out. 'Your sister?'

Dane frowned. 'Stepsister,' he corrected, with heavy emphasis on the first word.

'Thank you,' Jenny told him with awful politeness. 'You saved me the trouble of explaining that there is absolutely no blood tie between us. Thank God.'

'Wasn't it unfortunate for us that your father and my mother had no more sense than to start a second marriage at their age...'

'Oh, it certainly was unfortunate for me,' Jenny said sweetly. 'As for you—well, I hear you aren't doing badly at all.'

Dane's face darkened, and Jenny almost panicked. It wasn't safe to remind Dane that, had his mother not married Richard Ashley, he would probably be running one of the dough mixers at the bakery rather than being its manager. In fact, if it had not been for her father's second marriage, Jenny told herself fiercely, she would never have met this officious fool who now had the right to call himself her stepbrother. It would have been no great loss.

'You always did throw the first punch so nobody could sneak up on you, didn't you, Red?' Without waiting for an answer, he turned to Steve. 'If your lunch break is over, Steve, shouldn't one of us be in the plant? I'll walk Jenny up to the hospital and then I'll be back. I trust you were going to see your father, Red? Or did you just come for the funeral?'

Jenny sputtered, 'You son of a…that's my father lying up there in that intensive care unit!'

Dane shrugged. 'You've forgotten it conveniently enough for the last five years. See you later, Steve.'

Steve look at his boss with a trace of anger, but said only, 'Will you be staying long, Miss Ashley?'

'I really don't know,' she said tightly, not looking at Dane.

'Till Richard is better, no doubt,' Dane said curtly, then added thoughtfully, 'or buried. Unless, of course, he has enough sense to throw her out today.'

Jenny watched Steve till he was out of earshot, then turned angrily to Dane. 'You always enjoyed airing our quarrels in public, didn't you?'

'I didn't see you holding any intimate information back.'

She ignored the interruption. 'And ordering everyone around—you get a positive kick out of that. Well, I'll decide how long I stay and when I go, and you won't get me to leave this town an instant sooner than I want to.'

'You're quick to interpret my motives, aren't you? Look, Red…'

'My name is not Red!'

'It's an ingrained habit. Look, Jennifer, if I had anything to say about it, Mother would never have called you at all.' He started down the gravel path, the dog penitently trailing at his heels.

'Obviously. At this point I might still be able to upset your applecart. Or should I phrase it more appropriately? I could put my hand in the cookie jar that you've grown to think of as all yours.'

'So now we get down to real motives. You want to be sure your inheritance is safe.'

Jenny dug her fists into her pockets to keep from hitting him. 'It's got nothing to do with inheritances. I'm worried about my father.'

'Pardon me for not believing you, but you haven't wasted much concern over him in the last few years. Now just as soon as it looks like there might be money in it, here's little Jenny. Complete with her mother's approval.'

'And how did you conclude that Rosemary approves?'

'It's obvious, Jenny. You wouldn't risk her good-will on the chance of your father taking you back.'

'I do have a mind of my own,' she said coldly.

'I doubt it. At any rate, when Richard had this attack, Mother insisted that you must be notified. I'm amazed that she knew where to find you, and even more amazed that you actually came. But since you're here and I can't get rid of you…'

'Do you mean that you haven't considered murder yet?' she asked flippantly.

'At least a thousand times in the ten years since I met you, Red. Don't push me. You are not going to upset Richard any more. I won't let you pull off the tearful reunion scene and talk him into reinstating you in his will and then take off and leave him with another burden of guilt as you did after you had that fight with him.'

'It's the bit about the will that really bothers you, isn't it, Dane?'

He paid no attention. 'I don't care if you stay ten minutes or two months…'

'I can guess which one you'd prefer!'

'But you'll promise me that you won't quarrel with him. Or else you'll go now, and I'll tell him you were unfortunately unable to make the trip. What will it be?'

'You'd like it if I left, wouldn't you? It would clear the way for whatever little schemes you have worked out.'

'How that brilliant man acquired such a blind spot

where you're concerned, I'll never know, Jenny. It was probably the same thing that attracted him to your mother.'

'Just leave my mother out of this, Dane. What happened to that college degree in chemistry Daddy financed for you? Did you prefer cookie dough to noxious chemicals after all?'

'I'd give anything to get back into those—as you call them—noxious chemicals. Baking bread and cookies for a living—God!'

'It's such a pity that you can't go back to your chosen profession. We'd all love the idea. But I don't imagine Daddy will be back to work soon, will he?'

'I wish you'd get it through your head that a coronary occlusion is not a stroll in the park,' Dane told her. 'I had to quit my doctoral program to run the company when he had his first attack, and it was small potatoes compared to what this one looks like.'

'I suppose he was paying for that degree, too.'

'You suppose wrong.'

Suddenly Jenny registered what he had said. 'His first attack? He's had more than this one?'

'So you were listening after all. Amazing! Yes, a minor attack—if there is such a thing.' He walked on a few steps. 'Five years hasn't improved your personality, has it?'

'It has nothing to do with time. It's strictly a matter of the people I have to be around.' She turned at the hospital door. 'The fascist in Intensive Care should let me in now, so I'll run along. Is there anything else I should know?'

'Mother told him you were coming, so it wouldn't be too much of a shock,' Dane told her.

'You didn't consider the possibility that it might be a pleasant shock?'

'Not for an instant. And not even pleasant shocks are good for heart patients. Keep that in mind, Red. No scenes. Dinner is at seven, by the way.'

'You aren't letting this upset your schedule, are you?' she said sarcastically.

Dane shrugged. 'Everybody has to eat.'

'Well, I'm staying at the inn. I won't be at the house at all.'

He was unconcerned. 'In that case, dinner will be whenever you want to walk to the dining room and order it. I'll talk to you later.'

'Not if I see you coming,' Jenny retorted.

RICHARD ASHLEY'S FACE still carried the slightly blueish tinge that indicated insufficient heart action, and Jenny's stomach ached as she got her first good look at him. He lay weakly in the high bed, the guard rails pulled up, his oxygen supply bubbling beside him, and an intravenous drip monotonously feeding into a vein in his forearm.

He's an old man, she thought. The hair that had been frosted lightly at the temples five years ago was all white now. He was nearing sixty, she calculated quickly. He hadn't exactly been young when she was born.

'Hi, Daddy,' she said gently, reaching between the rails to pat his arm.

'Jenny.' It was little more than a breath. He lifted a hand weakly, and she took it between both of her own. 'I'm sorry I have to greet you this way.'

'Daddy…' She wanted to cry, to tell him how she hated to see him this way, how sorry she was that the five long years had stretched out between them, a headstrong girl and a man too proud to show his hurt. But Dane's stern face appeared in her mind, one eyebrow raised, as he had told her, 'No scenes, Red.' So she squeezed her father's hand and said nothing at all.

'You'll be staying, won't you, Jenny? Just seeing you is the best medicine I could have.'

'That depends on how fast you get well. I can't stay too long, you know. I will have to get back.' She didn't want to make any promises. Jenny hated promises; too many of them, she had found, were impossible to carry out.

'Just a few days?' The disappointment in his eyes shocked her. 'At least till Christmas, Jenny?'

'I don't know, Daddy. That's two weeks.'

He tried to smile. 'Got a boy-friend you can't stand to be away from?'

'At least a dozen.' Her voice was teasing. 'I'm never going to limit myself to one.' Or would she? she wondered. She stared at her bare ring finger, wondering if Brian's diamond would soon gleam there.

He hadn't actually asked her to marry him, but she thought it was only a matter of time. Perhaps if she spent a few weeks in Twin Rivers it would give them both a chance to think about it.

Richard, weak as he was, had not been fooled by her feeble joke. 'Someone special, Jenny? Would I like him?'

Jenny smiled. 'I think he's very special, and yes, you'll like him, Daddy.' Why had she said that? she wondered. In all probability, the two men would never meet. Brian was a junior executive in a big corporation, and he would have little to gain by getting to know Richard. Brian knew only people who might be of advantage to him.

Yes, Jenny thought, a couple of weeks in Twin Rivers, away from Brian Randall, might not be such a bad idea. It would give her a chance to think things over and realise whether she loved Brian or had just let him become a habit.

The dispirited droop of Richard's mouth nudged her to say, 'Maybe I can stay. I don't know. Don't worry about it, please.' Surely there was no harm in letting him think she might spend Christmas in Twin Rivers. There would be plenty of time for her to break the news if she decided to leave after he was better.

He was tiring fast. 'I expect you have a job you have to get back for. My daughter the advertising executive.'

Jenny laughed. 'It's public relations, Daddy. And I'm hardly an executive. I don't have any talent for writing those snappy ad slogans, but I could get good P.R. for Attila the Hun.'

He smiled weakly. 'Have you seen Margaret? She was anxious for you to get here.'

'No. I came straight to the hospital, and she had gone home. I'll see her later.'

He didn't press. 'What are you doing now, Jenny? Are you living with…'

He wouldn't even say her mother's name, Jenny realised. For the first time in her life she stopped to think about the shock it had been to him when Rosemary had left him with an infant child to care for. It had all happened more than twenty years ago, but it was still having its affect on him.

'No, Daddy. I have my own apartment, with a bunch of the girls I went to school with. Apartments are so terribly high-priced…' She chattered on.

A nurse tapped her on the shoulder. 'Sorry, Miss Ashley, your ten minutes are up.'

This one really sounded sorry, Jenny thought as she patted her father's hand. The shift had changed while Jenny had been down at the lagoons, and the fascist was gone.

Richard held on to her hand. His grip was pitifully weak. 'Don't go, Jenny. I'm afraid I won't see you again.'

'I can't stay, Daddy. They want you to rest now. But I'll be right down the hall, and I'll come back in another hour, just as soon as they'll let me.' She freed her hand gently.

He closed his eyes with a sigh.

Jenny paused at the desk, where the nurse was bending over a chart. 'Why are his visitors so limited?'

'It's just intensive care unit policy, Miss Ashley. You'll see a quick change when he's moved out in a room in a few days. This unit is a depressing place to be.'

Jenny felt a little better. 'I'll be in the waiting room.'

'Very well. If he asks for you, we'll come and get you.' The nurse gave her a genuine smile. 'I'm expecting Dr Grantham to be in soon; would you like me to ask him to stop by the waiting room?'

'Would you, please? I'd like to see him, if he has time.' Jenny walked down the hall to the little waiting room, feeling for the first time that her father was in good hands.

The room was furnished in reds and blues—strong, cheerful colours that somehow made her feel even less cheerful. She curled up on a sofa and yawned. She was exhausted after that long drive; her tiny economy car was not intended for comfortable travel. Margaret had called late last night, and Jenny had been on the road at dawn.

She yawned again and closed her eyes. Maybe she could snatch a nap. The nurses must be used to having families camping out in this room, waiting for the next time they could see their loved ones.

But all she could see was Dane Sutherland's face,

stern and brooding, his grey eyes wary and—was hateful the word she wanted?—as he had looked down at her. That was understandable, she told herself. After five years, Dane certainly didn't want her coming back, just when he had achieved what he had wanted. Richard Ashley was an invalid, and Dane was in control of the Ashley empire. Jenny wasn't dumb; she could understand why he would resent her reappearance. But there had been a time when he hadn't felt that way about her. The last time she had seen him, before she ran away...

She shook her head and tried to force him out of her mind. He wasn't important, after all—wasn't even a part of the family as far as she was concerned. But seeing him again had stirred old memories. She put her head back against the chair cushion and allowed herself to remember.

She had been twelve and Dane seventeen when their parents had married. And though Jenny had been resentful of the new additions to the family, she and Dane had managed to make peace of a sort between them. Having some interests in common had helped. Dane had taught her to ski when they'd all vacationed in the Rocky Mountains, and he'd taught her to dance and how to turn down a date without causing hurt feelings.

Having a brother had certain advantages, she had had to acknowledge. But as they got older the quarrels grew, until it had seemed that they were in a continual argument whenever they were in the same room.

Jenny had never understood why; she just knew that about the time she turned fifteen Dane had stopped being helpful and easy to talk to. She had concluded that he was out to get all he could from her father, and that he was now seeing her as a rival. And so they quarrelled whenever they were together, until Margaret had headaches and Richard left the room and the housekeeper yelled. Nothing anybody said could seem to stop them.

And then there had been that day five years ago—the last time she had seen him.

There was a bustle in the corridor and she opened her eyes as a grey-haired man came in, his lab coat hanging open. 'Hello, Jenny,' he said. 'May I sit down?'

'Of course, Dr Grantham.' Her tone was affectionate. This was the man who had treated her chickenpox, and had set her broken arm the time she fell out of the top of the apple tree, who had taken her seriously when the first signs of teenage acne developed and she had panicked.

'You've changed in five years, Jenny,' he said, settling himself comfortably. He put Richard's chart on the table in front of him and laced his fingers together at the back of his neck. 'Not all for the better, either. Your eyes are shadowed. Is that natural, or is it worry over your father?'

'Both, I guess.' She uncurled and sat up straight. 'How is he, Dr Grantham? Really?'

'Not all the test results are back yet. We won't

know much definitely until then. He has had a heart attack; there's some damage showing in his blood and his heart rhythms, but until all the tests are in we won't know how serious it is. He will probably be out of intensive care in a few days, home in another week after that, perhaps.'

'What about the future?'

'He'll be housebound for the winter, of course. It's unfortunate that he won't be able to get outdoor exercise, but the cold won't allow that. He may be a good candidate for surgery to bypass the blockages in his cardiac arteries. But even so, he'll still have the damage from the two attacks he's already had.'

Jenny closed her eyes and took a deep breath.

'He can't return to his normal pace for a long time, Jenny. He knew this was a possibility; that's why he turned the company over to Dane.' He studied her face, his eyes shrewd. 'That bothers you, doesn't it? That Dane's in charge of the bakery?'

She bristled. 'And why shouldn't it bother me? It's always been Ashley property. Now as soon as Dane's in charge, it doesn't even carry the Ashley name.'

'It is still Ashley property,' he told her bluntly. 'And if you'd been here, Richard would have turned it over to you.'

'I love my father, Doctor, but he never believed I could do anything for myself.'

Dr Grantham grunted. 'At any rate, Dane didn't want it. I'm sure Richard could have been persuaded to let you try.'

'Dr Grantham, I would never have had a chance, and there's no point in discussing it. And I didn't come here to be lectured about Dane's Good Samaritan instincts. I want to talk about my father.'

'Very well. You'll be staying, won't you?'

'Just for a few days. I told Daddy I might stay till Christmas, but I probably won't.'

Dr Grantham sighed and polished his glasses on his lab coat. 'What is there,' he asked finally, 'that is more important to you than your father's life?'

Jenny pulled both feet up on to the edge of her chair and clasped her hands around her knees. 'What do you mean? If you're trying to put the blame on me...'

'Of course not. It isn't your fault that Richard has had a heart attack. But he has had a great many anxious moments over you in the past five years. You could relieve his mind a great deal by staying here for the winter, by letting him see that you still love him, that you're still the daughter he adores. Five years without a word to him, Jenny—that was cruel.'

'It was five years without a word from him, too, Doctor. And why should he have anxious moments? He knew I was with my mother.' Jenny's voice was bitter.

'I imagine that's exactly why he worried,' Dr Grantham said dryly.

'You never liked her, did you, Doctor?'

'No. Never,' he said bluntly. 'I think it had something to do with the fact that when you were born

Rosemary wouldn't even look at you till you were bathed and dressed.'

Jenny shrugged. 'She has her failings…'

He gave a bark of laughter. 'Failings? Is that what you call it when a woman walks out on her husband and two-year-old daughter? Failings?' His eyes softened. 'Jenny, I don't want to quarrel about Rosemary. But tell me, what is more important to you than your father? Your job?'

She shook her head silently.

'Then you'll stay?'

'I don't want to.'

'You must. You're the best medicine he could have right now—having you back here, knowing that you're father and daughter again. You're all he has, Jenny.'

'He has Margaret and Dane—and he's managed very well with them for five years.'

'Perhaps. But you're his blood.' He looked at her thoughtfully, and mused, 'I remember how you rarely had a babysitter when you were tiny, because wherever Richard went he took you. He'd scarcely go anywhere that you couldn't be with him. And he would never have married Margaret if he hadn't been certain she'd be a good mother to you—no matter how much he loved her.'

'I could have done without the honour,' Jenny muttered.

'Could you? Really? I suspect you're a lot fonder of Margaret than you would ever let anyone see.' He let her think about it a moment. 'Won't you stay here for a few months—through the winter, until he's back on his feet? And then, if you must go, part friends and stay in touch with him? Should that be too much to ask?'

'No.' It was sullen.

'Good girl!' He got to his feet.

'I didn't say I was staying, Doctor. I just said it shouldn't be too much to ask.'

He stopped at the door and looked back at her, disappointment in every line of his face. 'Jennifer Ashley, if you aren't compassionate enough to take pity on an old man who thinks the universe revolves around you, then you aren't good enough to have his name.' And he was gone.

She sat unmoving for several minutes, and then the nurse came in. 'Your father is asking for you, Miss Ashley,' she said.

Jenny stared at the wall for a few more moments, then slowly rose and followed the nurse back down the hall to Intensive Care.

CHAPTER TWO

THE SNOW WAS falling as Jenny walked from the University Hospital high on the hill down through the campus and past Ashley Hall of Business, donated to the University by her grandfather. She crossed the wooden bridge that arched over the lagoon and threaded her way through the downtown area. The stores were still open and busy with after-work shoppers. The early dark had fallen, and the wind bit through Jenny's jacket.

She had seen her father twice more; the last time he had said she looked exhausted and had told her to go home and rest. It was ironic, she thought, that even in his present condition he was more concerned about her than about himself.

What Dr Grantham had said had struck deep; Jenny had spent the afternoon remembering the truth of what he had reminded her about. Her father had always been within call, it seemed. Though she knew it wasn't possible that he had always been with her, still she couldn't remember a time that her father hadn't come when she called his name.

With his devotion to her over the years, was it too

much for her to do to stay the winter while he recovered?

She wanted to stay. She had been lonely for her father, missing the closeness they had always shared. There was nothing preventing her from staying; her job was an entry-level position and despite what she had told her father, she would not be missed in the least if she didn't return. And Brian would understand; he'd have to, because there was nothing definite between them. Her mother would probably not be so understanding, but Rosemary would have to deal with any disappointment she felt. She'd had to do that before when Jenny had not done as Rosemary wanted.

And yet, Jenny told herself, it would be next to impossible to live in Twin Rivers as long as Dane Sutherland was under the same roof. It wouldn't do her father any good if all he heard was quarrels. She couldn't realistically imagine herself and Dane actually declaring a truce and living by it. They'd scarcely had a good look at each other today before they'd been headfirst into a quarrel.

But she wouldn't give Dane the satisfaction of driving her away, either. After all, it was her father, and her home. If her father wanted her to stay, and if Dr Grantham said she should...

'Jenny! Jenny Ashley!'

She turned in surprise as a small-boned brunette pushing a pram came up behind her. 'I thought I couldn't mistake the colour of that hair,' the brunette said.

'Alison!' Jenny exclaimed. 'Are you still living here?'

Alison wrinkled her nose. 'Yes. My plans to star on Broadway got a little messed up when I fell in love. With one of your old boy-friends, by the way. Jim Riley.'

Jenny glanced down at the pram. 'And this must be little Jimmy, I take it?' The baby's head was covered by a light blanket patterned in yellow ducklings.

Alison laughed. 'No, it's little Molly. Look, do you have time for a cup of coffee? I've been shopping all afternoon and Molly's tired and I'm tired and I'm dying to talk to you. Are you back to stay?'

'Just for a few days.' She glanced at her watch. 'I can take time for coffee, but I don't want to be out of touch for too long, in case they try to find me.'

'Then let's go in here.' Alison negotiated the pram through the doorway with the ease of long practice. She sank on to the bench in one of the comfortable booths and sighed. 'Christmas shopping is no fun when you have a baby tagging along, let me tell you,' she said.

'Christmas shopping was never any fun,' Jenny retorted. 'How old is Molly?'

'Eight months.' Alison removed the blanket, revealing the baby's round face and tiny mittened hands, all that showed of her outside of the pink fur snowsuit. 'I thought you were never coming back to this town.'

'I never intended to. If Daddy hadn't gotten sick, I'd still be happily forgetting that I ever saw Twin Rivers. But you could have invited me to the wedding. If you were going to marry my very best boyfriend, you should have let me know.'

'I wasn't taking any chances on him changing his mind at the last minute. One look at you again and he'd have been gone. You have snow in your hair, Jenny. Surely you haven't forgotten that winter around here requires a hat?'

'No, I haven't forgotten.' Jenny put a hand up to her hair, remembering that Dane had taken her stocking cap and had not returned it. Well, she could buy another. She certainly wasn't going to hunt him down to ask for its return.

The waitress poured their coffee. 'How is your father doing?' Alison asked, reaching for her spoon.

'He looks awful. But Dr Grantham says he's doing fine.'

'Everybody over at the bakery is really concerned about him,' Alison said. 'Jim said they collected money yesterday to send flowers.'

'Does Jim work there now?'

'Yes, he's the personnel manager. He works directly under Steve Whitman, who's the assistant manager.'

'And who works directly under Dane. I've met Steve.'

'Fast work on somebody's part,' Alison remarked. 'It's too bad that it happened right at Christmas. I suppose you'd made plans. But at least you'll be able to enjoy the only fun season Iowa has.'

Jenny sipped her coffee. 'Rosemary is spending Christmas on a cruise ship in the Caribbean.'

'Oh, well, cancel what I said about fun seasons here. Rotten luck, Jen.'

Jenny shrugged. 'It can't be helped. I hadn't decided whether I wanted to go or not.'

Alison just looked at her in disbelief.

'Is any of the rest of our crowd still here?'

'You mean your old boy-friends?' Alison giggled. 'Not many of them. A couple are working over at the university, and there are two or three more at the bakery. But most of them headed out for the bright lights, as you did. Are you married, Jenny?'

'No. Not even engaged. I'm disappointed in you, Alison. Remember? We were going to be career girls. You were the next Sarah Bernhardt and I was a budding White House press secretary. And look what happened to us!'

'Well, whenever you get to the White House I'll come and visit. Aren't you even serious about anybody?'

Jenny sipped her coffee. 'One here and there. No one I can't live without.'

Alison sighed. 'That probably means you're waiting for him to propose. I can't wait to hear all the details.' Molly stirred and started to cry. Alison reached into a diaper bag and put a dummy in the child's mouth. Then she took a hasty sip of her coffee. 'Darn. I think Molly is letting me know that she wants to go home. Which is probably a good idea, or her daddy will have the cavalry out looking for her! When your father's better, I'll have you over for lunch, Jenny, so we can catch up on all the gossip. And let's see—there are a lot of things going on this month. Small town stuff, of course, but better than nothing. Would you like to take some of them in with Jim and me?'

'I might as well. But I don't know how long I'll be around, so don't count on me.'

'All right, I won't count on you. But you can't leave Twin Rivers without telling me all about your man.'

'Why are you so certain there is one?' queried Jenny.

'Because you've never been without one.' Alison wrapped the baby up again and trundled the pram back out on to the street.

Jenny sat very still, her hands wrapped around the cup to absorb the warmth of the liquid. Alison had been her closest friend for years. They'd double-dated, shared girlish confidences, assessed every man who had moved into Twin Rivers according to their own secret scale. It would be nice to have Alison again. Then she reminded herself that she probably wouldn't be in town long enough.

She sighed in relief as she entered the warm lobby

of the small steamboat gothic inn, a relic of the days
when the larger of the two rivers that ran through the
city was navigable and passengers had debarked from
riverboats in hoop-skirts and buttoned shoes.

She stepped up to the desk and asked for her room
key. She'd have to go up and unpack; she had just
dropped off her luggage and signed the registration
slip earlier.

The clerk looked confused. 'But…but you've
checked out, Miss Ashley,' she stammered.

'I most certainly haven't,' Jenny snapped.

'But your luggage was called for, and your bill was
paid—'

Jenny's eyes narrowed dangerously. 'Would it happen to have been Dane Sutherland who took care of
all this?' she asked softly.

'Yes, Miss Ashley, it was. He said…'

Jenny wasn't interested in what Dane had said.
'Did he leave my car, or did he take that too?'

'He was driving his own, miss.'

'Thanks for everything,' she said sarcastically, and
ran down the front steps and around to the parking
lot. Her little car was still there, and she spun the tyres
as she pulled out on to the street.

The overbearing demagogue had gone too far this
time, she fumed as she drove up the long hill to where
the Ashley house stood. She was not going to let him
order her around!

In other circumstances, the big grey clapboard
house with its black shutters and warmly lighted bay

windows might have brought nostalgic tears to Jenny's eyes, for it was the only home she had known till she was seventeen. But she was too angry to let sentiment get in her way as she stormed up the steps to the back door. She stopped with her hand on the knob, for from inside came a deep voice! Dane's.

'She's no Miss America, that's sure,' he said. 'I don't know why Mother insisted on calling her— she's probably caused Richard to have another attack this afternoon.'

Jenny pulled the door open. 'Perhaps Margaret insisted because it is, after all, my father who's lying up in the hospital bed,' she retorted, advancing to the centre of the room.

Dane looked at her unconcernedly over the handful of peanuts he held, then selected two and crunched them between strong teeth. 'As I was saying before I was so rudely interrupted, Muriel,' he said, turning back to the housekeeper, 'I don't understand why Mother thought Red could do any good around here.'

'If you're so sure I'm useless, why didn't you let me stay down at the inn?' Jenny asked. 'I would have been perfectly happy there.'

'Appearances. Mother didn't want it to get back to Richard that the Prodigal Daughter hadn't come home after all.' He flipped a peanut to Finnegan, who seized it in mid-air.

'Well, just show me my luggage and I'll be happy to get out of here. And I'll tell Daddy it was all my idea and nothing to do with his precious other family.'

'Sorry. There isn't a room left for you at the inn.'

'I'm sure you arranged that,' said Jenny bitterly.

'How did you guess? I'd hate for you to miss out on anything. Since you're here, you might as well be right on hand to make sure you'll get your share.'

'You make me sound like some kind of vulture!'

Dane looked up from his peanuts, suddenly sombre, 'Aren't you?'

The woman at the stove finally spoke. 'All right, you two. I'd have thought by the time you grew up you'd quit fighting, but if you can't stay out of each other's way I'll have to take a hand. Dane, Richard isn't dying, so you can quit the gallows humour. Here, take your mother's tray up to her room so the poor child has something to eat before she goes back to the hospital.' She spooned a serving of a steaming casserole on to a plate and set it on a tray that already held a salad and a glass of milk.

Dane obeyed the plump housekeeper without a word. Muriel watched him go and turned to Jenny. 'And you, young lady,' she said. 'The next time I hear a nasty word from you about Margaret, like that crack about your father's other family, I'll wash your mouth with soap! Take it out on Dane all you want—you're two of a kind. But don't do it in front of Margaret. She never did anything to hurt you.'

Jenny's silence was a kind of apology. 'I'm still not staying in this house,' she said.

'Yes, you are. And that's the last I want to hear of that sort of nonsense,' Muriel said briskly. 'Jenny, if you don't get that chip off your shoulder, I'll guarantee Dane will knock it off. Now you're going to have to co-exist with him until Richard is better, and it isn't going to make it easier on anybody if you're fighting all the time.'

'He started it,' Jenny muttered.

'Now if that doesn't sound like a three-year-old, I never heard one,' Muriel said sighing. 'I'll settle him down. Now let me have your promise to stay here. We both know you can't afford the inn, anyway. Nobody can. Go on and get freshened up. And you'd better hurry if you want your dinner while it's hot.'

'I feel ten years old again,' Jenny said.

'That's half the idea,' Muriel agreed.

Jenny climbed the carpeted stairs from the front hall, thinking about how Muriel had always lovingly bossed her around. Jenny's earliest memories were not of her mother, whom she could not remember at all from her childhood, but of Muriel.

Her room was just as she had remembered it, the walls a warm apple green, the four-poster bed already invitingly turned down. Soft patterned curtains were pulled across the long windows that looked out over the town. Jenny sighed softly. It felt good to be back in this room that had sheltered her childhood.

She unpacked her luggage, hanging dresses in the enormous closet and filling the numerous drawers with jeans and tops. She was surprised that nothing in the room had been changed; even the clothes she had left behind were neatly folded into the drawers. Muriel's idea, she wondered, or Margaret's?

She was wrapped in a terry robe, ready for her shower, when there was a tap on her door. She called permission to enter.

'How pretty you've grown, Jenny.' The soft voice held an apologetic note, as though Margaret questioned whether she would be welcome. 'I'm on my way back to the hospital, and I wanted to see you before I left.'

Margaret wore a red pantsuit which emphasised her platinum hair. It was shorter than she had worn it five years ago, and it looked as if she'd been to the hairdresser that afternoon. But then Margaret had been a hairdresser for years, and she never looked less than elegant. The thought of Margaret looking tatty was laughable.

And, Jenny told herself, looking at Margaret with new eyes, Muriel was right. Margaret had never done anything to hurt Jenny. She had always tried to build a trusting relationship between them; it certainly wasn't Margaret's fault that Jenny had been a spoiled teenager unwilling to accept a stepmother.

Margaret smiled tentatively and held out a hand to Jenny, as if unsure what the response would be. Jenny surprised even herself. She took Margaret's hand and bent to brush her stepmother's cheek with her lips.

'I'm so glad you've come, dear,' said Margaret. 'It's a great relief to have you here.'

And for the first time since she had met Margaret,

Jenny did not look for a hidden, sarcastic meaning under the words.

'I don't know how much help I'll be,' she said.

'Just being here is all the help in the world.'

'Do you want me to come back with you tonight?'

'Oh, no. I won't stay there all night, since we're so close to the hospital. And you look exhausted. Why don't you spend tomorrow morning with him?'

'I am tired,' Jenny admitted. 'That's a long drive. He looks so weak, Margaret. It frightens me.'

'All we can do is trust his doctors and time, Jenny. I must go—but I wanted to tell you how important it is to me that you've come. And to Richard, of course.'

Jenny noticed that Margaret had tactfully not included Dane. That was all right with her, she decided. She'd just as soon pretend that he didn't exist, and if he felt the same about her, that was fine.

'Muriel said to tell you that she was going on home, but the casserole is in the oven and the salads are in the refrigerator,' Margaret said. 'She isn't working full-time any more, so we fend for ourselves some these days. And we aren't very elegant any more. I hope you don't mind.'

'Dressing for dinner has never been my favourite occupation,' said Jenny. For the first time she stopped to realise that dinner would be a twosome.

She went to take her shower as soon as Margaret left, and shrugged off the idea. Why worry about it? she decided. Maybe Dane would be thoughtful enough to go out to eat.

But a few minutes later when Jenny came down the stairs, dressed in tailored slacks and a ruffled blouse in a warm, creamy peach colour that accented her complexion, Dane was waiting for her in the door-way to the big living room.

He watched her descend the stairs, his gaze making her aware for the first time of just how tailored her slacks were, and said when she reached the lower level, 'Can I get you something to drink? Do you still have your adolescent passion for draught beer?'

She was determined not to let him needle her, 'A Martini will be fine, if that's what you're having.'

He raised an eyebrow. 'You really have joined the advertising game, haven't you?'

'It's public relations, not advertising. There's a large difference.'

'Probably not when it comes to three-Martini lunches.'

'Don't you ever put your best foot forward?' Jenny asked curiously, reaching for the glass he held out.

'If I did, you'd trip over it, Red,' he said lazily.

Jenny sipped the Martini and said, 'I wish you wouldn't call me Red.'

'Sorry. It just seems inevitable; every time I look at you it reinforces the idea.'

She groped for another topic of conversation. 'I know Margaret said the rule about dressing for dinner has relaxed, but I hardly expected jeans and sweaters.'

'If I'd known it would bother you, I'd have worn my faded flannel shirt,' said Dane. 'There are some of us who don't get our kicks from seeing how much we can spend on clothes.'

'If that's a nasty crack aimed at Rosemary...'

'Actually it was a nasty crack aimed at you,' Dane corrected silkily.

Jenny ignored the interruption. 'Do you own a suit these days?'

'I can't remember. I'll look some day and let you know.' He didn't sound interested.

Jenny set her glass down on the coffee table. Out of the corner of her eye she saw a reddish figure lumber to its feet. The Irish setter plodded across the room.

'I'd watch that glass closely,' Dane warned. 'Finnegan is next door to being an alcoholic.' He took a thoughtful sip from his glass. 'If I was around you all the time, I might be tempted to join him.'

'I'm flattered that you even notice me,' Jenny said gently. 'Do you mean this dog really likes to drink?'

'Of course. That's how he got his name. The day I brought him home, your father was having his whisky and soda and turned his back, Finnegan drank it and then had to sleep it off by the fire. Richard named him, actually, from the song. His full name is Finnegan's Wake.'

Jenny turned back the pages of her memory to her father singing the old Irish song and hummed the first few lines. 'With a love of the liquor he was born?' she murmured.

'Exactly. It fitted the puppy like a glove. Even

though he does prefer beer and pretzels, he'll drink anything. Let's have dinner. It's a shame to let Muriel's casserole dry out.'

The kitchen was warm and bright. Dane got plates and cutlery while Jenny took the casserole out of the oven.

'Let's just eat here, shall we?' he asked, straightening the bright chintz place mats on the round oak table. 'The dining room seems a little elegant for a pick-up meal. Unless you need to have the atmosphere?'

'This is fine.' Jenny decided not to react to his assumption that her mother's chosen mode of life was also hers. It would do no good to tell him that Rosemary's lifestyle bored her. He would never believe her; no one did. Alison hadn't believed that anyone could turn down a Caribbean cruise. Even Brian refused to believe that she wasn't content with the social swirl. What none of them realised was that she needed to be busy, to be doing something worthwhile.

'Did you decide how long you'll be staying?' Dane asked as he held her chair. The question was not as offhand as the tone of his voice.

'Not yet. But Daddy won't kick me out.'

'Perhaps your employer won't let you take time off,' he speculated.

'I'll stay as long as Daddy's health is in danger.'

'Of course, money isn't any problem, is it? I keep forgetting that with the fortune your mother married, you have no need of minor sums like a job would provide.' His eyes flicked over the frilly blouse.

Jenny ran a gentle hand over the sleeve. 'Yes, it did come from Paris,' she said. 'It was a birthday gift. And if you're trying to drive me out, Dane, you can stop any time. I plan to stay as long as I like, no more, no less. And you won't change my mind.'

'How long is that?'

She shrugged. 'Interpret it any way you like. You will, anyway, so why should I help you out?' She sampled the casserole.

Dane didn't answer, and Jenny was determined not to make the first move. She ate her dinner, studying him covertly, satisfied that he seemed uneasy and fearful that she might stay in Twin Rivers. Perhaps Dane wasn't as untouchable as he liked to think he was.

He would be delighted to have her leave, because then there'd be no question that he would remain in control of the bakery as long as Richard was unable to work. It might do Dane good to be kept in suspense, wondering just what she was going to do.

And, she thought, in the first flush of success, a five-years-older Jenny would not have any great difficulty in dealing with Dane Sutherland. He was just a man, now, and Jenny had plenty of experience in dealing with men. She could handle this one too. All she had to do was outlast him. With a sudden glow of satisfaction, she savoured Muriel's Bavarian cheesecake. This might even be fun!

They put the plates in the dishwasher and went back to the big living room. Dane put a stack of records on the stereo and came to sit beside her. 'A quiet evening in the bosom of the family—so to speak,' he commented as the first record dropped.

'You've never been part of the family as far as I'm concerned,' Jenny said coolly. 'You're strictly an accident.'

'Your personality hasn't exactly improved with the years.'

Jenny shrugged. 'I'm not a vintage wine. And I seem to remember you once thought I was attractive.'

'Do you mean the last Christmas you were here? That was strictly your body, Red—not your mind.'

'Thanks. You do my ego wonders!'

'Any time.' He grinned. 'I'll be delighted to keep you cut down to size.'

Maybe it would be best to clear the air, Jenny thought. 'That episode was no big deal, anyway,' she said. 'We were just a couple of kids—there were hormones running loose all over the place. It wasn't important.'

'You don't sound convinced that it wasn't important,' Dane disagreed. 'Now I considered it quite important. At the time, of course. With a little perspective, I feel differently about it. Now I realise you were just a teenager trying out your new skills.'

'Are you saying I was a tease?' she demanded.

'Of course. All teenage girls are. Not to mention the outfits you used to wear,' Dane continued calmly.

'I don't think you owned a bra when you were seventeen. At least I never saw you wearing one.'

'You couldn't have been looking.'

'Believe me, I was looking,' he said dryly. 'And I have a question. If that little episode wasn't important, why do we both remember it so well?'

'Probably because it was so unpleasant.'

'I don't think either of us considered it unpleasant at the time. Would you like a demonstration, just to remind you?'

'No, thanks. If I want to be mauled, I'll visit the zoo and climb in with the grizzly bear.'

'What kind of men have you been associating with in the last five years, Red?' he drawled.

'Not your kind, thank heaven!'

'Perhaps you're right, Jenny. Maybe we should forget all that and concentrate on the present. Your body is still very attractive.' His eyes roamed appreciatively over her. 'Attractive enough that I could put up with your shrewish temper.'

'My shrewish temper? Have you looked in a mirror lately?' She closed her eyes, put her head back against the couch cushion, and asked, sounding bored, 'Why on earth do you think I might be attracted to you?'

'This,' Dane said softly, and kissed her. His mouth was warm and gentle, moving sensuously over hers. He released her lips to let his mouth trail across her cheek to a tiny earlobe, nibbling at the small pearl earring. With an effort, Jenny lay perfectly still, not reacting to him at all. That should make him mad, she thought. If Dane thought he was the irresistible force, he was about to run into the immovable object.

He kissed her again, and Jenny pushed him away. 'Sorry, you don't turn me on,' she said flatly. 'I'm not seventeen any more. So leave me alone.'

'At least that was calmer than the last rejection I got from you,' he commented. His hand, resting on the nape of her neck under the curtain of her hair, was warm as he massaged the tense muscles. 'What's the matter, Jenny? You can't have it both ways, you know. A minute ago you assured me that I've never been a part of your family. Yet when I kiss you, you act as if I'm committing a crime.'

'There are a lot of men who are not related to me that I don't want to kiss,' Jenny pointed out. Her voice was a bit breathless. She wished he would take his hands off her. It was becoming increasingly difficult to stay still.

He smiled. 'I'm sure that's true. You don't act like a woman who has ever been truly awakened.'

'I suppose you think you could do it.'

His eyes flicked lazily over her. 'Shall we try it, Jennifer?' His hand cupped her throat and his thumb rested gently on the pulse at her collarbone. 'Your little heart is just going wild, isn't it? What's the matter? Are you afraid I'll kiss you again? Or are you afraid I won't?'

She pushed his hand aside. 'I think I'll go up to bed. I'm really tired.'

He raised an eyebrow. 'Are you running away?

You're going to have to stop that.' His husky voice
was a promise. 'I never thought you were a coward,
Red.'

Jenny fled up the stairs and shut her bedroom door
firmly. She leaned against it, her breath coming in
gasps. Obviously it wasn't going to be as easy as
she'd thought.

She had forgotten that Dane wasn't the sort to stand
by and allow anyone to take his playthings away
without a fight, and he wasn't above using any means
that came to hand. Jenny's mere presence was threatening his possession of the bakery; he would do his
best to immobilise her or drive her away. Dane had
learned to fight as a child growing up on the wrong
side of town, and he wasn't likely to change his style
to conform to what Jenny expected.

'Well,' she told herself philosophically, 'now
you're prepared. You know his plan of attack, and it
will be perfectly easy once you get yourself under
control.'

Brave words. But would she be able to control herself? She didn't understand why a man whom she
disliked—no, hated—as she hated Dane could still
have such an impact on her.

She closed her eyes and sagged against the door,
remembering against her will that last Christmas—the
winter she had been seventeen.

Dane had been twenty-two then, a senior in college
and only home for holidays. He had come home to

spend Christmas, and the day he was ready to return to campus, he had come to her room to say goodbye.

They had had an argument that morning—one of a continual series since the moment he had come in the front door ten days earlier. As best Jenny could recall, she had asked him if he would set her up with a date for his fraternity's next dance, and Dane had said she was too young to date his frat brothers. No matter how she pleaded, he had been adamant. So she had retreated to her room and pouted, refusing even to come down to say goodbye.

When he came into her room and asked lightly if she was going to kiss him goodbye, she had been polishing her toenails, and she had ignored him. He had been teasing about the kiss, she thought; Dane's kisses were a mere brush on the cheek, and though Richard and Margaret had been married almost five years, Jenny could count on one hand the number of times Dane had kissed her.

But her refusal to recognise his presence seemed to aggravate him; he had pelted her with pillows until she had retaliated, then he had wrestled her on to her bed and held her there and taken his kiss.

And an innocent, juvenile brush of the lips it had been, too, Jenny thought, and her cheeks reddened in embarrassment for her younger self. How very naïve she had been at seventeen!

But then she had turned her head at the instant Dane had moved to release her, and as their eyes met there had been one blinding instant of realisation, then all sense was swept away as their lips met again.

That kiss had been far different, Jenny remembered guiltily. She could still feel the fire that had swept through her body in response to his demanding caresses. They had been far past the kissing stage when she had regained her common sense and pushed him away. What would have happened had Richard and Margaret not been downstairs was a question Jenny asked herself sometimes in wakeful midnight moments.

What she had said then she could not remember, for she had been nearly hysterical with fear—not only of him but of her own reactions. But she knew it had struck him hard, whatever it was she had screamed at him, for he had turned absolutely white and walked out, and she hadn't seen him again. He had skipped his usual weekends at home, pleading heavy studies, and at spring break he had gone to stay with friends. He hadn't come home yet when she had had the fight with her father and run away. And, she had to admit, she might not have taken such a drastic course of action if she hadn't known that summer was near and Dane would be coming home to work in the bakery.

He was right, she admitted. It was still important to her, if only because she didn't understand why it had happened. And down deep, no matter how much she told herself that it was only a matter of a couple of kids, she didn't quite believe that it was only that.

Jenny sighed and stepped away from the door. She

might have found the weak spot in Dane's armour, and she might be able to exploit it by simply staying in Twin Rivers; but it looked as if he had also found the chink in her defences.

CHAPTER THREE

JENNY CAME DOWN the stairs into the living room in a swirl of pleats, her black velvet evening cape draped over her arm.

Dane was lounging in a chair near the fire with one hand resting on the top of Finnegan's head, listening to the Symphonie Fantastique on the stereo. He looked so comfortable that it irritated Jenny. 'Why do you listen to that gloomy stuff?' she asked.

'And you with the expensive education,' he mocked. 'Some day when I have all kinds of time I'll teach you to appreciate Berlioz. He isn't a gloomy composer, merely moody.'

'I'm afraid I don't appreciate the difference.'

Dane looked her over and raised an eyebrow. 'Don't we look fancy tonight?' he asked. 'That's considerably more dressed up than you've been to go to the hospital before.'

'That's because I'm not going to the hospital to-night.'

Dane didn't seem to hear, but his eyes were intent on her slender figure, studying the way the fine soft white fabric of her dress draped, the line of her legs in the sheer tights and high-heeled sandals. He seemed to focus on the delicate gold of the bracelet on her right ankle. 'So where are you going instead? You'll notice I'm not crazy enough to think you're dressing up to stay home with Finnegan and me.'

Jenny crushed the urge to tell him it was none of his business. 'I'm going to the play over at the University.'

He made another sweeping assessment of her from head to foot. 'Not alone, I presume?'

'No. Steve Whitman is picking me up.'

'You aren't wasting any time getting your social life under way, are you?' he commented. 'You've only been home four days, and Richard just came out of intensive care this morning.'

'Yes, and since Margaret's staying with him this evening, he suggested I go out. So there!' She felt like sticking her tongue out at him.

'And Steve just happened conveniently by, I presume?'

'No, he asked me several days ago. But I didn't decide to go until I knew Daddy would be out of intensive care.'

'I see. Does Steve know you're almost engaged?'

Jenny turned to stare at him. He looked relaxed and at ease in the big chair, but she wasn't fooled. He was like a coiled snake waiting to strike at her. She wondered how he knew about Brian; she thought she had been careful not to talk about him.

'Whether I'm almost engaged or not is strictly my own business,' she said coldly.

'And the lucky man's, of course.' He scratched Finnegan's ear, draped across his knee, and said thoughtfully, 'Why do we always refer to the man who gets the girl as the lucky man? Frankly, this one has my sympathy. What's his name?'

Jenny ignored him. 'I'm not exactly going on a date anyway. Steve's picking me up, but we're going in a group.'

'The lucky man might have a different opinion,' said Dane.

'He might—but I don't think so. At any rate, you certainly have no right to an opinion about it. And would you stop calling him the lucky man!'

'Only when I know his name.'

'Make one up,' Jenny said shortly.

'How about Harvey? No, that makes me think of a rabbit.'

'You don't have to refer to him as anything at all.' Jenny draped the evening cape over the back of a chair.

'Won't he be upset at you for dating Steve?'

'I told you, it's not really a date. And I'm not engaged. I'm not committing any crime to go out for a Saturday evening!' Jenny's voice was beginning to rise, despite all her efforts to keep her temper under control.

'You sound very defensive about dating Steve—all this business about it really not being a date at all. Would Harvey be upset?'

'Of course not. Brian is very understanding.'

'Brian—so that's his name. He sounds like the perfect man, Red. I'd watch out for him if I were you—he's inconsistent.'

She couldn't help rising to the bait. 'Inconsistent? How?'

Dane smiled. 'Well, he may be the perfect man—but he certainly didn't wait to find the perfect fiancée, did he?' He eyed the pillow she had caught up, and said, 'I don't recommend you throw that, Red. I'm afraid I'd be tempted to retaliate, and you know where that always gets us.'

Jenny flung the pillow back down on the couch.

'I must have been wrong that first night to think that you were as innocent as you seemed,' he said thoughtfully. 'Would you like to convince me?' He make a quick move as if to get to his feet.

Jenny moved quickly to put the width of the room between them, and only then realised by the warm glow in Dane's eyes that she had reacted precisely as he had hoped she would. He hadn't actually moved an inch, she realised, but the warmth of those grey eyes felt like an actual caress on her skin. How could he make her feel naked just by looking at her?

'Have you decided how long you'll be staying? Just how long can Brian live without you?'

'I don't know how long I'll be here.'

'Or maybe the question is, how long can you live without him? He hasn't even called you yet. Doesn't that worry you, Red?'

Before Jenny could answer, the Westminster

chimes pealed, and she went to answer the front door. Steve stepped in, shaking a few flecks of snow off the fur collar of his overcoat.

'I've never seen a winter start out like this one,' he muttered. 'It's snowed every day since Thanksgiving, and no let-up in sight. By the time spring comes they'll have to call in an archaeologist to find us!'

'Your blood just hasn't had an opportunity to get accustomed to the Iowa winter,' Dane said lazily. 'Now to us natives, this is pure pleasure, isn't it, Red? Half the charm of the Iowa winter is the relief when you come in where it's warm.' He stretched his feet out closer to the fire.

'I'd just like to know how long it takes to get used to the weather,' said Steve. 'Seems like two years should have done it.'

'Give it another twenty,' Dane advised.

'I think I'll go back to Arizona instead.'

Dane shrugged. 'Whatever you like. I happen to like variety.' His eyes were resting on Jenny. I'll just bet you do, she thought.

Dane looked back at Steve and asked, 'Where are you taking Jenny tonight?'

'I told you, Dane,' Jenny pointed out. 'And I'm grown up. You don't need to act like a nineteenth-century chaperone.'

Steve said, 'The University Theatre group is doing a new abstract play. I thought Jenny might like it.'

'Sounds a little highbrow for Red,' Dane observed.

'And how would you know what highbrow is?'

Jenny flared, and instantly regretted it, for Dane merely grinned.

'Well, if you don't appreciate the classical composers, dear...'

'I do, most of them. I just don't happen to like Berlioz, for heaven's sake!'

Dane didn't pursue it, merely turned back to Steve to say, 'And what time will you have Jennifer home?' He crossed the room to the stereo and turned the volume down.

'Oh, for pity's sake, Dane, stop acting like my...' Jenny stopped dead.

But Dane finished the sentence for her. 'Like your big brother? Are you sure you can cope with me if I do, Red? You might find yourself with your hands full.'

'We're going with Jim and Alison Riley, Dane,' Steve added.

'I'm sure Brian will be relieved,' Dane mocked.

Jenny glared at him.

'Who's Brian?' Steve asked as the door shut behind them.

Jenny ignored the question. 'It certainly isn't any of Dane's business who I'm going to the play with, Steve,' she told him flatly as they descended the front steps to his car. He helped her in and walked around to slide behind the wheel.

'It's only natural for Dane to be concerned, Jenny,' he said mildly. 'After all, your father is in hospital, and he feels responsible for you.'

'Like heck he does!' Jenny snapped. 'How do you all think I got along for five years with neither Dane nor my father checking out all my boy-friends?'

Jim and Alison were waiting, so the argument ended before Steve had anything to add. Alison slid into the back seat and leaned across to brush Jenny's cheek with a kiss. 'I'm glad you could come tonight,' she said. 'How's your father?'

'Daddy's much better today, and they've moved him out of intensive care. They don't think it was a severe attack.'

'I'm glad of it. I wanted you to come.'

'And Margaret's with him tonight, so I didn't think it was really necessary for me to be there too. Hi, Jim. How's my very best boy-friend?' Jenny laughed as Jim Riley's hand came down hard on her shoulder.

'You know better than to make my wife jealous, Jenny,' he teased. 'We might have been able to get away with something if you hadn't ruined it by making her suspicious.'

The play was definitely abstract, and Jenny had trouble keeping her mind on it. Steve was enjoying it, though; he was sitting with an arm possessively arranged across the back of her seat, but all his attention was on the stage.

At intermission, she and Alison walked through the crowded lobby to the ladies' room.

'Are you having some trouble with Steve?' Alison asked. 'If he's acting up, I'll…'

'Nothing like that,' Jenny said dryly. 'I'm just having a little difficulty with the play. Literature was never my best thing. Whose idea was this, anyway?'

'Steve's, actually. Jim happened to mention knowing you. So…'

'Steve's a nice guy,' said Jenny. 'And if I could get him to think in terms of an Alfred Hitchcock film now and then, I'm sure I could really grow to like him. But I'm irritated with him right now because he actually explained to Dane where he was taking me and what company we'd be in.'

'He's a gentleman. If that bothers you, you're really crazy, Jenny.' Alison thought about it and then nodded wisely. 'What's really upsetting you is that Dane's playing the heavy-handed big brother, right?'

'You might say.'

Alison shrugged. 'He's been acting strange for a long time, ever since he came back to take over the bakery. I think he's still miserable about having to give up his own profession. Chemistry is his love; his heart certainly isn't in baking bread and cookies.'

'He's got you fooled, too?' Jenny queried. 'His heart may not be in baking bread and cookies, but you won't see Dane giving up control over that business without a power struggle. After all, it's what he's been after for ten years. The minute Daddy and Margaret were married, Dane was starting to plan.'

'Give him a break, Jenny! Dane never had the advantages most of our crowd did, but he's made a great deal of himself.'

'Yes, and he's done it all on Ashley money,' Jenny

said tartly. 'Intermission's almost over. We'd better go back.'

The second half of the play was just as ungraspable as the first, and Jenny, bored, started to look around over the audience. Steve was absorbed in the action, and Alison, who was sitting on her other side, seemed to be nearly as interested. It was the theatre-in-the-round, with the stage extending into the audience and little of the standard theatre setting about it.

The lights came up a little on the stage, and off to her left Jenny saw Dane, with an elbow resting on the arm of his chair and his chin propped on his hand. As he watched, he tipped his head towards a honey-blonde girl sitting beside him. Whatever he said must have been funny, for the girl laughed lightly. And inappropriately, Jenny thought, for it was far from a comic moment in the play.

He had some nerve, she thought, to act as if it was a crime for her to be going out, when he obviously had already made plans himself. She leaned towards Alison. 'Who's the blonde girl with Dane?' she whispered.

Alison's eyes were intent on the stage. 'Suzanne Sumpter. Remember her from high school?'

'But you didn't even look over there,' Jenny protested.

'Didn't have to. I saw them when we went out for the intermission. But even if I hadn't, she's the only blonde he's dated in the last year.'

'She never used to be a blonde,' Jenny mused.

'That's why I didn't recognise her. Her hair was always kind of a mousey brown when we were in school.'

'There are a lot of things Suzanne is now that she never used to be,' Alison added. 'Like Dane's secretary.'

'Well, that does put her on the scene, doesn't it? Is he serious about her?'

'How should I know? I doubt it; Dane has more sense than that. I'm trying to watch the play, Jenny. It's hard enough to make any sense out of this without you chattering.'

Steve frowned at her too, and Jenny subsided, thinking how unfair it was that Dane had proved to be right after all—the play was considerably too highbrow for her taste. It aggravated her, as she looked across the stage again, that Dane seemed to be enjoying both the play and the company very much indeed.

It wasn't until they were back at Jim and Alison's house that they returned to the subject. Alison was making coffee and Jenny was slicing a chocolate layer cake when she repeated, 'Is Dane serious about Suzanne?' She licked frosting off her finger.

Alison plugged the percolator in. 'They've certainly been spending enough time together, and I'm sure she'd like for it to be serious. But Dane doesn't confide in anyone. Why do you ask?'

'I guess they're the same type,' Jenny explained.

Alison looked up in surprise. 'Dane and Suzanne? You're joking!'

Jim wandered in and leaned over his wife's shoulder. 'What are you two gossiping about?'

'I thought you took the babysitter home,' said Alison.

'Steve volunteered. Since his car was warmed up, I let him.' Jim picked up a section of cake that had tumbled off the plate. 'And I just checked on the little darling and she's sleeping soundly with a dry diaper. Now what were you saying about Dane and Suzanne?'

'Jenny thinks they're made for each other.'

Jim put both arms around his wife's waist and nibbled her earlobe. 'Why? Because they both originated on the wrong side of the tracks?'

'Oh, something like that,' Jenny said vaguely.

'I couldn't disagree with you more. Suzanne spells culture with a capital K,' Alison sniffed.

Jenny sidetracked the argument. 'How do you like working for Steve, Jim?'

'He's a nice guy to work for. He's willing to delegate responsibility, and that's worth a lot. Of course, Dane gives Steve quite a bit of authority, because Dane would much rather be over at the university in a chemistry lab.'

'That's what everybody keeps telling me. Why don't I believe it?' Jenny mused.

'He's darn good at it, too. He's developed some products that he holds patents on,' said Jim. 'But Dane does everything well.'

'I suppose next you're going to tell me that the

bakery is running better than ever before,' Jenny said acidly.

Alison shook her head. 'You sound like a broken record on the subject of Dane, Jenny. You're obsessed, and as far as you're concerned the man won't ever be able to do anything right. So let's drop the subject. Will your father be home in time for Christmas?'

'We all hope so. Dr Grantham says another week in hospital will be enough. But he'll be recuperating all winter.'

'Well, you'll at least be coming to the company Christmas party next week, won't you? And we're having a New Year's Eve party; you'll have to come to that. It looked like such a hassle to hire a sitter for the evening that we decided to stay home and let our friends come here this time.'

Before Jenny could reply the back door opened and Steve came in.

'Just in time,' said Alison, unplugging the coffeepot as it finished perking. 'Jim, if you would like to stop distracting me so I can carry these things to the dining room...'

IT WAS WELL AFTER midnight by the time Steve took Jenny home. The wind had come up in the meantime, and fingers of snow were blowing across the streets and settling in drifts in the gutters. The cold ripped through Jenny's velvet cloak. Whoever had described it as suitable for winter wear had obviously never spent December in Twin Rivers!

Steve parked the car next to the front steps and turned towards Jenny. 'Thank you for going to the play with me, Jenny. That's one of the things I miss most here in Twin Rivers; so few people really appreciate theatre.'

Jenny felt a little guilty about letting him think that she had appreciated the play. But what harm could it do to leave him the illusion? she asked herself. 'It's a shame that so few people take advantage of the opportunities the college presents,' she said.

'That's true. And not only the theatre but the concerts and other fine arts. Last fall there was a marvellous man here—a tremendously talented violinist. And no one seemed to care. Half the auditorium was empty.'

'Well, at least the other half was full,' Jenny put in gently.

'That's true. You do look at the positive side of things, don't you, Jenny? I'm so glad you are here. Twin Rivers seems like a different town. A pity you can't stay till Christmas.'

'Oh? Who told you I wouldn't be here for the holidays?'

'Dane said you were leaving.'

Jenny started to a slow burn. So he was so confident of himself he was announcing her departure, was he? If Dane Sutherland thought it was so easy to get rid of her now that her father was better, just let him try! 'I think Dane must have misunderstood,' she said coolly. 'I've made no plans to leave yet. I may even stay till spring.' Especially if Dane wants me to go, she thought.

'Perhaps I heard him wrong. I'm glad you're staying, Jenny. I really want to get to know you better.'

'I like you, too, Steve.' Jenny was a bit troubled. Should she warn him about Brian? Surely that wasn't necessary; one evening hardly meant that the man was head over heels in love with her. She shivered and gathered the velvet folds of her cloak around her. 'In any case, it's too cold to sit here and talk. I'd ask you to come in, but I don't want to risk waking Margaret. She's been so exhausted the last few days I'm starting to worry about her.'

He was already shaking his head. 'It's so cold I don't think I want to have to go out in it again, Jenny. All I want right now is a warm room that I don't have to leave for at least eight hours. Maybe next time.' But he got out of the car and came around to help her out. At the top of the steps, he took her key and unlocked the door. 'I had a pleasant evening, Jenny,' he said, turning her to face him, one hand under her chin. 'Maybe next week we can take in the new Italian film downtown. It's supposed to be the best picture of the year.'

Jenny smiled, wondering vaguely if his taste in movies resembled his ideas of good plays, but then she nodded. 'I'd like that, Steve, if Daddy's progress allows it.'

'I'll call you. I've enjoyed this evening more than any other since I came to this cultural wilderness. I hope we can do it again, Jenny.' He pulled her close for a quick, chaste kiss, and waited, the perfect gentleman, until she had closed the front door behind her before returning to his car.

Jenny dropped her cape across a chair in the living room and stretched her hands out to the fire which still flickered, hardly more than a bed of embers, in the grate. Steve was likeable, she decided. Even if their taste in plays didn't seem to be similar, he was a pleasant companion. They probably had many things in common; it would be fun to find out what they were. She just must be certain not to let Steve get too serious about her.

She yawned and went up to her room, being careful to be quiet so she didn't wake Margaret as she passed the door of the master bedroom. Dane's room lay beyond her own, and she didn't even look down the hall towards his door. The house was quiet, so he must be asleep, or else he hadn't come home yet. Perhaps he was still entertaining Suzanne. It wasn't hard to guess how, she thought, and admitted to a twinge of surprise herself. Despite what she had said about Dane and Suzanne being two of a kind, she had never expected that combination. Dane had always dated the brilliant girls, the good girls, and Suzanne had been neither.

In her own room, Jenny hung the velvet cape carefully in the closet and dropped the white dress over a chair to be dealt with tomorrow. She wrapped herself in a long fleece robe in her favourite apple green and went into the adjoining bath to brush her teeth.

Steve was not only nice, but he was considerate and attractive, she thought, dabbing on moisturiser with a cotton wool ball. She remembered his concern for her by the lagoon the first day she had been in town when Finnegan had knocked her over. Yes, definitely a man worth knowing, she decided. Was she being fickle, she wondered, to be interested in Steve? Or was she just being sensible to look out for herself by considering what Steve could do for her? He might even be a good ally to help her find out just what Dane might be trying to hide. She was thinking about that as she came back out of the bathroom, humming a little tune under her breath.

'You sound pleased with yourself.'

She jumped. Dane was lounging on her four-poster bed, sprawled across the rumpled eiderdown, a mug in his hand, dressed in the same bulky knitted sweater and dark slacks he had been wearing earlier. The bulk of the sweater and the brilliant graphic design knitted into the pattern emphasised the width of his powerful shoulders, tapering to the slim line of lean hips. It wasn't exactly formal wear for the theatre, Jenny told herself, and then in all honesty had to admit that avant-garde university theatre wasn't the Metropolitan Opera.

'What are you doing in my bedroom?' she demanded.

'Can't you see? I'm relaxing on your bed. Are you

pleased with the progress of your conquest?' Dane asked.

'I don't know what you mean. And get out of here. I'm tired and I want to go to bed.' Jenny pulled the belt of the fleece robe tighter around her waist.

'What's stopping you?' Dane asked softly. 'It's a big bed. There's plenty of room for both of us. We can both be comfortable while we talk. Unless you'd rather have a pillow-fight?'

'Do you have to be so distressingly crude?' she snapped.

He looked surprised. 'Why are you distressed? I thought you said it was no big deal—that little affair five years ago. Didn't you tell me we were just kids, and it was just hormones?' When she didn't answer, he stretched lazily and rolled over on to his side. 'Actually, I came in to give you a message. Brian called a while ago. He didn't sound too pleased when I told him you were out on a date.'

'I'm sure you enjoyed giving him all the details,' Jenny said shortly.

Dane looked hurt. 'I didn't want to lie to the man, Red. After all, if he might become my brother-in-law…'

'He won't,' Jenny said curtly.

'Steve is a fast worker, isn't he?' Dane said admiringly. 'One date and you break up with your boyfriend.'

'I didn't break up with Brian! But you're not my

brother, so he couldn't be your brother-in-law, even if I marry him.'

'Even if? You didn't sound that doubtful before, Red.' He yawned. 'But I feel cheated. Who knows, Brian might turn out to be my best friend.'

'I have my doubts,' Jenny said sarcastically.

'Now how would you know? I'm a very tolerant person; I have all kinds of strange friends. At any rate, it must have been a successful evening. Steve definitely had you branded as his personal property, from the way he had his arm around you all evening. I think he'd like to be a very good friend. And I don't think Brian would appreciate that in the least.'

Jenny shrugged. 'I suppose you told Brian all about your speculations.'

'Not yet. I have to keep something back for blackmail. Besides, I was too concerned about it myself to worry about what he would think.'

'I don't see what concern it could be of yours.'

'I was just interested in knowing whether my assistant is so far up in the clouds over you that I won't be able to rely on him any more. Judging by the goodnight, though, I'm not worried. Actually, you could have been a little more generous with him; a couple of kisses wouldn't have hurt you. Or were you thinking about the objections Brian might make if he found out?'

'You were watching while I said goodnight to Steve?'

He raised the mug and sipped from it. 'I wouldn't

call it watching, exactly,' he parried. 'I was observing from a scientific standpoint. And if Steve is head over heels, as I judge he probably is, on the kind of evidence I saw tonight, then I understand why you were looking so all-fired pleased with yourself.'

'If you're trying to upset me, you can quit now, Dane.' Jenny walked across to the window and pulled the corner of the curtain. 'And you can get the hell out of my room.'

Dane raised a dark eyebrow. 'I'm only here because I thought you might want to share some confidences. Frequently girls do after important dates, you know. They need a father figure to confide in when they feel confused.' He set his mug down on her bedside table and folded his hands as if prepared to listen all night. 'Was this an important date? And do you feel confused?'

'If I was choosing a father figure, you wouldn't be it!' Jenny turned back to the window, pretending not to care if he left or not.

'Have you decided how long you'll be staying?'

'No, but I hear you have. Steve said you'd told him I would be leaving next week.'

'Did I? It must have been wishful thinking on my part.'

Try as she might, Jenny could find nothing wary or suspicious in his tone. 'What's going on that you're so anxious for me to leave, Dane?' she asked curiously. 'Whatever it is, I'll find out about it.'

'Perhaps it would be thoughtful of me to just tell you how things stand,' he mused.

'It certainly would.'

'But I think I'll wait and let you figure it out.' He was silent for a few moments, watching her impatience as she tapped her fingers on the little piecrust table beside her armchair. Then he added thoughtfully, 'Somebody has to take care of you, Red. Actually, I was only watching your goodbye tonight because I didn't want anything unfortunate to happen to you while you were in my care—so to speak. Richard would never forgive me. To say nothing of Brian.'

Jenny lost her temper. 'Oh, would you just stop pretending to be my damned big brother!'

'I thought you'd never ask.'

He rolled off the bed and on to his feet in one catlike motion, and before she could dodge out of his way he was across the room and was holding her firmly, his hands clenched on her upper arms.

She had to look a long way up into his face, it seemed, for barefoot she hardly reached to his chin. Dane had always been tall, but it seemed to Jenny that he had suddenly got even taller than she remembered.

'All right, you've proved your point,' she said angrily, struggling a little.

'No, I don't think I have,' he said, giving her a little shake. The humorous note that had been in his voice was gone. 'I wish you'd make up your mind. You act as though I'm beneath your contempt, hardly fit to speak to. Yet you expect that when it comes right down to it I'll remember I'm supposed to be your brother and that means I have to keep my hands off you. I've waited around for you to make up your mind for just as long as I intend to wait, and now I'm warning you, Jenny, I have never considered myself to be your brother, and you might just as well watch out, because I'm not going to act the part any more, Brian or no Brian!'

She looked up at him, almost stunned, her brown eyes enormous in a shock-white face. He said something muffled under his breath and bent his head.

'No!' Jenny breathed.

Dane ignored her protest. His mouth covered hers almost tentatively, as though careful to savour the first taste of her lips. It was a gentle kiss, almost teasing in its softness. His hand came to cup the back of her head and to stroke the length of the tumbled red-gold hair. The tie belt of the fleecy robe had come loose, revealing a deep V of Jenny's creamy skin, and Dane turned his attention to the shadow between her breasts, his hand gently stroking, teasing, caressing.

Jenny drew a ragged breath, and as if he could read her mind, Dane uttered a little groan deep in his throat and kissed her again, not gently this time but hungrily, like a starving man who has been handed a loaf of bread.

Something deep inside her seemed to shatter, and she pressed herself against him, kissing him back with every ounce of strength she possessed, her hands finding their way up under his sweater to caress his skin, hot to her touch.

Suddenly he let her go, and she was startled to find herself clinging to him for support to prevent herself from falling. 'Brian would kill you for this,' she murmured, hardly hearing her own voice.

'Are you certain he wouldn't kill you instead? Seems to me you were enjoying it too, my dear.' He set her aside and said politely, 'And what makes it his business, anyway, Jenny? If you're not engaged to him, that makes it all right for anyone who wants to play.' He reached for a lock of her hair and let it slide through his fingers. 'And I do so want to play, darling.'

He set her aside and said coolly, 'I've decided what I want from you, Jenny. Perhaps you should make up your mind as to just what you want from me.' He ran his fingers through his dark hair and walked out of the room.

CHAPTER FOUR

JENNY SIGHED, yawned, rolled over, and looked at the clock on her bedside table. Then her eyes snapped wide open and she flung the blankets back. She had overslept. If she was going to early church with Margaret, there was barely time to throw on her clothes.

She rummaged through her closet and pulled out a pale pink wool skirt, then searched until she found the matching mohair sweater in a dresser drawer. In her haste she snagged a fingernail in a new pair of pantyhose, creating an enormous run, and had to start again. But finally she was dressed, the red-gold hair was brushed out into a stream down her back, and she was running down the stairs.

Margaret was in the breakfast room, neatly dressed as she always was, this time in well-tailored blue wool. She was drinking coffee and reading the Sunday supplements, looking as if she'd been up for hours.

'How do you manage to look so calm on Sunday morning when I'm running around like crazy? You must have stayed up all night just to make me look bad,' Jenny accused lightly. In the last few days, they had come to a new understanding of their relationship. Now that Jenny no longer needed someone to keep her under control, they had discovered a growing fondness for each other.

Margaret looked up with a smile. 'You don't look rushed to me; you look very lovely. Would you like a cup of coffee?'

'Do I have time?' Jenny sank into a chair.

'Certainly. We'll just go to the later Mass today. I looked in on you an hour ago, but you were sleeping so soundly that I didn't have the heart to wake you. It looked to me as if sleep would be a much more spiritual experience than church!'

Jenny yawned. 'You might be right at that, but I don't want to miss church today, I haven't been very faithful about going the last few years, but this may be the only Sunday I'm here.'

Margaret poured her coffee and handed the delicate china cup and saucer across the table. She looked unhappy. 'Are you still determined to leave us again so soon?' she asked.

'I'll stay till Daddy's out of hospital. But really, Margaret, it just isn't going to be very comfortable around here. And don't pretend that you don't know what I mean.'

'Yes, I know. And I've talked to Dane about it. I just don't understand why you two can't declare a cease-fire, I wish...' She sighed, 'Was the play good last night?'

Jenny reached for the cream and sugar. 'No, but

the company was pleasant. I saw Dane there. Did he enjoy it?'

'I didn't even see him this morning. He left a note saying he was going up to his cabin. He must have left fearfully early, though.'

Jenny had a feeling she knew just how early, but she didn't want to be the one to tell Margaret. She wouldn't be surprised if he had left right after that little scene in her bedroom. She smiled a tiny, secret smile. So Dane hadn't been as calm as he would have liked to pretend. He'd had to leave the house. Well, it beat taking a cold shower, she supposed—especially in December. She was glad that he hadn't been as cool as he'd pretended; she herself had been a long time finding sleep.

'I didn't know anything about a cabin,' she said. 'Is it his own little retreat?'

'Hasn't he told you about it? He's so proud of it I'm amazed you haven't heard all the details. He bought the property several years ago—just a little clearing out in the middle of nowhere, about fifteen miles west of town.'

Jenny thought about it. 'Out by Oak Drive Park?'

'Yes, just north of there. Heavens, Jenny, I'd forgotten that we used to take you picnicking out there. He just built the cabin last summer. It isn't entirely finished; he's doing most of the work on it himself. I often think Dane would be happier if he could just go live out in the middle of a wilderness somewhere,' Margaret added.

And the rest of us could breathe easier, too, Jenny told herself. But she said sincerely, 'He isn't exactly the executive type, is he? Or even the sort I think of when I imagine a research scientist, Dane just doesn't seem to belong with tiny test-tubes and precision measurements.'

Margaret poured herself another half cup of coffee. 'You could have knocked me over when Dane was ten and he confided that he wanted to be a chemist. If he'd said he planned to be a forest ranger, I'd have believed it. Somehow it always seemed to me that he would be more comfortable with animals than chemicals.'

'And more comfortable with either than with people. I'd like to see his little cabin,' added Jenny.

'Don't be offended if you aren't invited,' Margaret warned. 'I've only been up there once. Dane says he needs a place that he can call his own, and I must admit I agree with him.'

'It isn't at all ordinary for a man who's nearing thirty to be living in the same house with his parents,' Jenny murmured.

'Yet that's the only arrangement that's really practical. So he spends most of his weekends up at the cabin. He's only been home for the last few days because of Richard. There's no phone up there, and he didn't want to be out of touch.'

'So he spends his time alone up there. Is he happy?'

'I don't think so. But he doesn't talk to me about it. He says he plans to move up there in the spring.'

'Perhaps if I decide to stay he'll move now,' Jenny commented.

Margaret smiled. 'I doubt it. He gets too much pleasure out of aggravating you! Last fall several of his buddies went up there, and almost all of them came home with deer.'

Jenny's stomach turned. 'They hunted deer? Those beautiful creatures?'

'Those beautiful creatures, as you call them, do a lot of damage to trees and farm fields, Jenny. Why do you think so many hunters come into Iowa to hunt in the fall? It's because all our deer are corn-fed. Not intentionally, of course.'

'I couldn't eat a morsel,' Jenny declared.

Margaret gave her an odd look. 'You like that summer sausage that Muriel has in the refrigerator, don't you, Jenny?'

'Of course, but... That isn't... Is it?'

'It's venison, from the deer Dane brought home last fall.'

'That makes me ill!' Jenny exclaimed in horror.

'Sorry, I probably shouldn't have spoiled it for you. But if you're wise, you won't tell Dane how you feel about deer.'

'Why not?' Jenny said stoutly. 'I'll stand up for what I believe in no matter who's on the other side.'

Margaret sighed. 'That's what I was afraid of,' she said. 'You know that it's never wise to argue with

Dane, and Dane knows how short your fuse is, and yet you're always in a fight. I wish I understood the two of you.'

'It's a waste of time to try, Margaret.'

The small brick church was almost full, but they found seats about halfway up the main aisle, and Jenny knelt on the needlepoint kneeler, remembering how as a child she had hated prayers before church because the needlepoint scratched her knees and made them itch. Her father had never understood, but Jenny remembered thinking that of course he couldn't understand; a man never had to wear the frilly dresses and spotless white ankle socks and black patent shoes—and consequent bare knees—that he had insisted were the proper dress for a little girl at church.

She smiled at the thought, and dragged her mind back to her prayers. Even though her father was much better, a few words to someone upstairs couldn't hurt.

The congregation was singing the opening antiphon when a man came up the centre aisle and paused beside her. Automatically Jenny moved over to make room for him, offering to share her hymnal. A strong brown hand gripped the book, and Dane said, 'I didn't expect you to be so anxious for my company, Red.'

Jenny was startled into silence for an instant, and in that moment Dane's firm baritone picked up the melody. 'Can't we at least declare a truce during Mass?' she whispered finally.

He grinned down at her and continued to sing, but he didn't make any further comment. During the sermon a young woman came in, and again they shifted to make room for her. It crowded them in the pew, and Dane's thigh pressed against Jenny's. She stirred uncomfortably, but he only gave her a sardonic smile and turned to extend an arm casually along the back of the seat.

He wasn't touching her, but his arm lay so intimately about her shoulders that she couldn't help wondering how it appeared to the people who were sitting behind them. 'Oh, stop it, Jenny,' she told herself fiercely. 'Just because you feel as if you've been branded it doesn't mean it looks that way to the others. And if anybody wonders otherwise, who cares? You won't be here long enough for them to form any opinions.'

The scent of his suede jacket seemed to surround and overpower her. It mixed with a musky fragrance that she remembered from last night—his aftershave. It was a relief when the service was over and they were back out in the cold wind.

Dane didn't seem to notice the wind. He stood, hatless, on the church's front steps, his dark hair ruffled, his gaze sweeping over the town that lay spread out below. Margaret tucked her hand into his arm. 'You didn't stay out at the cabin long, Dane,' she said. She sounded a little surprised.

'No. There are some things I have to take care of,' he said carelessly.

'I didn't expect you to be back today, so I thought Jenny and I would just have lunch at the hospital.'

'That's fine. I'll find something in the refrigerator. Don't worry about me.'

'Of course not,' said Margaret. 'I never do.'

Jenny heard the dry note in her voice. Margaret might be doing her best to keep it from Dane, but she was obviously worried about him. Jenny wondered if it was normal motherly worry, or if there was something else Margaret was concerned about.

Dane had heard it too. He looked down at his mother with a laugh, and for an instant the lines etched between his brows eased and his eyes were alight with humour. 'And that's a lie if I ever heard one, Mother,' he said.

Margaret refused to be embarrassed. 'At least it was a well-intentioned one,' she pointed out. 'It's far too cold to stand here talking. I suppose you'll be home this evening?'

'Some time,' Dane agreed. 'But don't wait on me for dinner.' He freed his arm gently and ran down the steps. At the bottom, a blonde girl lifted a hand and he went to join her. It was Suzanne Sumpter. She looked up and smiled at Margaret, but her eyes were hard when she looked at Jenny.

'Well,' said Jenny, and darted a look at Margaret, 'I don't remember Suzanne being a member of this church.'

'She wasn't,' Margaret returned glumly. 'Not until after she went to work for Dane.'

Their eyes met in a look of total understanding, then Margaret shook off her concern. 'I keep trying to remember he's a big boy now,' she said as they walked to the car. 'I almost wish sometimes that he'd move out of the house. At least then I wouldn't be able to worry so much about what he was doing.'

'Yes, you would,' Jenny told her. 'Probably more so.'

Margaret forced a laugh. 'I suppose you're right. Has anyone ever told you, Jenny, that you're very wise sometimes?'

'Never,' said Jenny. 'Shall we go straight to the hospital? I don't know about you, but my stomach is reminding me that my breakfast was nothing more than coffee.'

The luncheon special in the hospital cafeteria was stuffed peppers. Jenny inspected them and said, 'As a professional, I have to admire this sort of thing, Margaret. It's a marvellous promotion technique. In a couple of hours everyone who's eaten these things will be downstairs in the emergency room.'

'I thought you liked stuffed peppers. You used to eat them.'

'That was your recipe. It's a different matter entirely.' Jenny halfheartedly selected a bowl of steaming vegetable soup.

'I thought you said you were hungry,' said Margaret as they unloaded their trays. 'No wonder you stay so thin.' She sipped her coffee and said, 'You didn't even finish telling me about the play.'

Jenny shrugged. 'Not much to tell. I didn't get anything out of it at all. Steve and Alison enjoyed it; I think Jim felt about the same way I did.'

'How do you like Steve?'

'He's fine. I really do like him, and he asked me to a movie next week.' Jenny stirred her soup thoughtfully. 'The one I fell in love with was Molly. But she was asleep last night by the time we got back to Alison's house, so I didn't even get to play with her.'

'She's a charmer,' Margaret agreed. 'I kept her one weekend when Jim and Alison went out of town for a short vacation, and Richard really enjoyed her. He spent the whole weekend hanging over her crib.'

'Alison seems to be perfectly happy as a house-wife,' Jenny mused thoughtfully, 'but I didn't expect her to be one of the first ones married.'

'Neither did Jim, I suspect,' Margaret said dryly.

'I wonder if she'd let me take care of the baby some time,' said Jenny.

'She'd love it if you wanted to volunteer. I'd do it myself, but I'm afraid Richard won't be able to take having a baby in the house.'

'You really love babies, don't you, Margaret?'

'Show me a woman who doesn't. I wish Dane—or you, of course—would settle down and provide me with a few grandchildren of my own.'

'Now, Margaret!' scolded Jenny.

'Sorry, I did assure you that I'd never turn into the kind of woman who hinted around about that sort of thing. But I have to admit I'd like to have some grandchildren before I'm too old to enjoy them.'

'Even if they look like Suzanne Sumpter?'

Margaret sighed. 'Well—I hope that I'm open-minded enough to accept Dane's choice, whoever she is. But...'

Jenny giggled. 'Your bias is showing, Margaret!'

'I have to admit to a prejudice against unnatural blondes. If the colour of hair a woman is born with isn't good enough for her, what is?'

'But then you were lucky,' Jenny pointed out. 'You didn't even turn grey; you turned platinum.'

'That's true. Perhaps I need to reassess my attitude.'

'Not that I'm sticking up for Suzanne, you understand,' Jenny added.

Margaret smiled. 'Of course I understand,' she said. 'You don't want Suzanne as a sister-in-law, do you?'

'Not if I have anything to say about it,' Jenny agreed, and added to herself, even if I do think Suzanne is exactly what Dane deserves!

RICHARD ASHLEY looked up with a smile as his wife and daughter came into the room. 'Here are my two favourite girls,' he said, and reached behind him to plump his pillows. 'I was beginning to think you'd got lost.'

'Jenny's stomach was about to go on strike if she

didn't eat something, so we stopped for lunch,' Margaret told him, and stooped to kiss his cheek.

'Let me do that, Daddy,' said Jenny, shaking the pillows back into position. 'How are you this afternoon?'

'I'm delighted to be out of that tiny cubicle. Now I know why I never turned to a life of crime—I couldn't have stood the punishment if I'd been caught!' He patted her cheek. 'They brought me my own television set a few minutes ago. I feel as if I've won a prize.'

'Maybe if you get all A's on your report card they'll let you watch the basketball games,' Jenny agreed. 'If you promise not to get too excited, that is.'

'I can give up all the basketball; that won't bother me at all. I'm just afraid they won't let me watch the Super Bowl,' Richard grumbled.

'Heavens, that's weeks away,' said Margaret, settling herself comfortably and opening her handbag to pull out a ball of soft pink wool. 'By then you could be a cheerleader, Richard.' Her knitting needles started to click monotonously. 'What did Dr Grantham say this morning?' she asked.

'He hasn't been in. You might catch him yet.' He turned to Jenny. 'How was the date last night, young lady?'

He winked at Margaret. 'You know, Jenny, in my day we never paid any attention to what was happening on the stage.'

'Daddy!' Jenny pretended shock. 'To think that you and Margaret...! I'm devastated.'

'We were young once too, you know. Steve seems to be a pretty nice guy. But if he gets out of hand, you just let me know, Jennifer.'

'And what will you do?' she mocked gently. 'I can take care of myself, dear.'

'There is a certain amount of debate on that point,' her father murmured.

'Richard,' Margaret warned, 'don't get into an argument.' She shook out the tiny sweater, held it up for inspection, and reached for her yarn to start on the second sleeve.

'Is that for Molly?' Jenny asked. 'It's cute.'

'Yes. I'm trying to finish up all my Christmas gifts this week. It's the only good thing I've found about Richard being here—it gives me plenty of time to knit.'

'Speaking of Christmas,' Richard began, and was interrupted by a cheerful voice from the doorway.

'How are the Ashleys doing today?' Dr Grantham boomed. He came on in, turned a chair around, and sat down with his arms folded on the back of it, his eyes intent on his patient.

'About time you got here,' Richard complained teasingly.

'Even doctors get a morning off once a year. It's written into my contract.' He reached for Richard's hand and inspected the fingernails. 'Good colour there; your circulation has improved. How are you feeling?'

'As if I've been stepped on by an elephant.'

'That's perfectly normal. Your test results look good, and you're progressing very well. I think you can go home by the end of the week if you behave yourself, Dick. Celebrate Christmas at home. Quietly, of course.' He turned to Jenny. 'Have you decided to stick around for a while?'

'I haven't made up my mind,' Jenny said.

His eyes were sad. Before he could pursue the subject, Margaret said firmly, 'We'll handle it, Doctor. You and Edna are coming to our open house on Christmas Day, aren't you?'

'Wouldn't miss it for the world. But I hope you'll celebrate with a little less fanfare this year, for the sake of Richard's heart.'

'Of course,' Margaret agreed. 'But it wouldn't feel like Christmas without half of Twin Rivers dropping in for eggnog on Christmas morning, would it?'

'We've been having that open house for so many years, I think it would be more strain to cancel it,' Richard agreed.

'Now that I've conned my annual invitation, I'll be on my way,' said Dr Grantham, smiling, and set his chair back in place. 'I'll see you in the morning, Dick.'

As soon as the door closed behind him, Margaret laid her knitting aside. 'Since Dr Grantham has brought the subject up, Richard...'

Richard nodded and looked thoughtfully at Jenny. 'Have you made plans for Christmas, Jenny? You mentioned this young man…'

Margaret looked startled. 'What young man?'

'The one Jenny thinks is special.'

'I said he was special, but we've made no plans.'

'And Rosemary? I'm sure she had something in mind.'

It was the first time he had specifically mentioned Rosemary. 'Well, yes,' Jenny admitted. 'She's taking a Caribbean cruise this year.'

Margaret's mouth tightened, and she looked down at the mound of yarn in her lap, disappointment written in each line of her face.

Richard sighed heavily. 'I guess that settles it.'

'I didn't say I was going along, Daddy,' Jenny added gently.

His eyes gleamed. 'We hoped you'd stay with us a while, Jenny. I'm not trying to make you feel guilty, but we feel cheated that we haven't had you with us for so long, and we don't want to miss another Christmas with you.'

'And not just Christmas, Jenny,' Margaret said softly. 'We're selfish, I suppose, to ask you to stay in Twin Rivers, but we want to get to know you again. You've grown up, and we want to get acquainted with the new Jenny. We'd like it very much if you would stay as long as you can.'

There was no mistaking the sincerity of Margaret's voice. 'I knew that you wanted me to come,' Jenny said at last, 'but I didn't know if you really wanted me to stay. I thought probably you'd be delighted to see the last of me, as much trouble as I've caused you both.'

Margaret moved abruptly, the sweater sliding unheeded to the floor as she dropped to her knees beside Jenny's chair. She took Jenny's face between her hands. 'Darling, even at your most trying times, you were a precious part of our family. And as for wanting to see the last of you—there hasn't been a day in the past five years that I haven't wished to have you back.'

Jenny reached out blindly, and Margaret held her tightly, her cheek pressed against the soft red-gold hair. 'Jenny, please, you must believe me! Without you we're not complete. We desperately need to see you now and then, and to know how you're doing.'

Richard sighed heavily. 'I'm jealous of your mother, Jenny. It's hard for me to admit that she has any rights at all where you're concerned. And she's had you for five years. All I'm asking is a few months. Stay as long as you like—but that's up to you. Just let me get to know you again.'

Jenny reached for the box of tissues on the bedside table. 'Daddy, I'm sorry I ran away. It was cruel. And…'

'Jenny, what happened five years ago is gone. You're home now.'

She was touched that her father wanted her to stay, that he was practically begging her to remain in Twin

Rivers. She had missed close family ties; Rosemary didn't want to be bothered. And her job was unimportant! There were dozens like it, and she could always go back.

An idea flickered in the back of her head. There must be room for improvement in the company's public relations. If she could do that, it would provide an ideal way of finding out just what Dane was up to and preventing it—whatever it was—from hurting her father.

She nodded. 'Okay, you win,' she said, and smiled mistily through her tears. 'I'll stay, for a few months anyway. Providing there's something I can do to keep myself busy. Can you use a P.R. person at the bakery?'

Richard looked surprised. 'You don't need to work, Jenny. We'd like you to be our guest.'

She reached for her father's hand. 'And it would drive me crazy not to be busy with something. Let me say thank you that way, please, Daddy. It's something only I can do.'

He smiled. 'Of course, Jen. Anything you want.'

'What a happy group!' Dane's voice from the doorway was lazy. He strolled across the room and perched on the radiator cover. 'There are just a few things I need to talk to Richard about,' he said smoothly.

'Not business, I hope.' Margaret retrieved her yarn.

'I'm afraid so, Mother.'

'I thought that sort of thing wasn't good for heart

patients,' Jenny gibed. She perched at the foot of her father's bed.

Dane looked at her steadily for a few moments as if she were an insect on a display board. 'I don't want him to get out of shape.'

'I may decide not to come back to work, Dane,' said Richard.

'Oh?' Dane's voice was politely interested, and Jenny wondered if she really heard the note of anticipation that lay under the word, or if she was only imagining it. No, she told herself, it was there, but it was very subtle. Dane had been waiting for this moment for too long to be careless now.

'No, Margaret and I talked about it last night, and we decided that we'd like to take it a little easier in the future.'

'Do some travelling, perhaps, when Richard is better,' Margaret put in.

'We want to live at a little more relaxed pace,' Richard continued, and reached for Margaret's hand. 'I've been fortunate, in a way, I've had two warnings to slow down, and that's two more than most people get.'

'What about the bakery?' asked Dane.

Jenny shot him a cold smile. Trust Dane to be looking out for himself first, she thought. No expression of agreement, or regret—just a quick question about how he himself would fare.

Richard's eyes were sad. 'It's yours, Dane.'

'Daddy!' The word burst from Jenny's throat.

Dane grinned sardonically. 'Worried about your share, Red? Maybe you'd better explain to her that you took care of all that when you incorporated, Richard.'

'I didn't mean it the way it sounded, Daddy,' Jenny said grudgingly.

'Of course not,' Dane mocked. 'Would you like to tell us just what you did mean?'

She glared at him and refused to answer.

'See?' Dane gibed. 'I told you to stick around to protect your interests.'

'Dane, stop it!' snapped Margaret, with the weariness of long practice.

'I know you regret that you had to interrupt your education, Dane,' said Richard. 'You're a gifted chemist, but you're also a gifted manager, and I think you've grown happier in the last year. Am I right?'

Dane's eyes were on Jenny and the mocking light in his gaze was for her alone as he said, 'Oh, you're right, Richard. I've reconciled myself quite happily to staying at the bakery.'

'I'll just bet you have!' Jenny thought.

Dane saw her disgust. 'Breaks your little heart, doesn't it, Red?' he gibed.

'I can run it, Daddy,' she urged. 'You don't need Dane.'

'You already own a share of the stock, Jenny,' her father told her. 'When we incorporated part of it was put in your name and part in Dane's to satisfy the law. But I'm not going farther than that. I have a good manager who is right here and planning to stay in Twin Rivers—I'm not going to take it out of his hands.'

'How do you know I won't stay?' Jenny asked.

'What would Brian think of that, Red? Wouldn't he object to you commuting?'

Richard ignored the interruption. 'Dane will look after your interests as well as his own, Jenny.'

In the hope that some day they'll really be his own, Jenny sighed. She reminded herself that her father didn't understand what he was talking about. He saw no reason to distrust Dane. She crossed her legs and tapped her fingernails impatiently on the footrail of Richard's bed.

'I'll accept your decision for now, Daddy,' she said finally. 'But I'm going to do the best job I can, and then maybe we can let Dane finish his precious education.' She met his startled look and added, 'I have a new job, Dane. I'm going to be your public relations department.'

It was her turn to enjoy Dane's discomfiture. She watched the look of horrified disbelief spread across his face. But just as quickly as it had appeared, it vanished, and he was back in control.

'You don't have enough experience,' he said flatly.

'Then you'll have to see that she gets it.' Richard's voice was firm. 'She could be a valuable asset, Dane. She's right, you know—she may be valuable enough that you would have time on your hands.'

'That does sound tempting,' Dane mused.

Jenny knew that he was thinking of the experience he would make sure she got. There would be nothing pleasant, if Dane had the arrangement of it, that she was certain of.

Dane continued thoughtfully, 'And Red is giving up everything she's used to and staying in Twin Rivers.' He leaned back in his chair. 'Are you sure you can do it, Red? Certain you won't run out about the middle of January?'

So he was giving her thirty days to fail, was he? Jenny's backbone stiffened. She had the pride of the Ashleys, and she would not allow anyone—not even Dane Sutherland—to drive her out of her own family. She'd stay as long as she wanted to, and she'd learn the business, and she'd find out whatever it was that Dane was trying to hide, then she would be the one who called the shots.

She watched her father intently. He looked exhausted; he shouldn't be worried about business so soon. She would do all she could to ease that worry for him; she could at least use her power as a stockholder to make sure that Dane didn't walk off with any more of the Ashley money than he was entitled to.

'I'm absolutely positive I won't run,' she said.

Dane grinned and raised an eyebrow.

'Well, that's all settled,' said Richard, and the note of relief in his voice was almost as strong as the exhaustion that crept through. 'I think I need some rest now, if you don't mind.'

Jenny jumped up. 'Sleep well, Daddy. I'll come back this evening if you like.'

'No date tonight?' Dane asked.

'Only with Daddy.'

'Steve must be losing his touch,' Richard speculated. 'Margaret, my dear, stay a little while, please.'

Margaret moved her chair closer to his bedside. 'Only if you promise to shush and go to sleep. If you insist on talking, I'll leave so you have to talk to the walls.'

Dane followed Jenny out into the hall. 'I'll buy you a cup of coffee,' he offered.

'Are you trying to convince everybody what good friends we are? No, thanks, if I'm starting work tomorrow, I'd better get some things done at home.'

'It isn't necessary for you to start tomorrow,' he countered.

She shook her head firmly. 'I want to get myself entrenched as soon as possible. If I wait a couple of days, you'll find a way to keep me out.'

'Why are you staying in Twin Rivers, Jenny? I can't believe it's the money, not with everything your mother has, but I can't quite believe that it's anything else, either.'

'Oh, of course it's the money, Dane,' she said coolly. 'I wouldn't expect you to understand any other motive.'

He grunted as if he half-believed her. 'In that case, why don't we make it easy? Market value on your stock right now is about twenty dollars a share. I'll give you forty a share, cash, if you'll sign it all over to me and leave Twin Rivers by Christmas.'

Jenny stopped in mid-step, in the centre of the hallway. 'And where would you get the money? I suppose you'd be delighted to be rid of me for ever so you can complete your takeover. But I'm not going to co-operate, Dane, I'm going to stay, and I'm going to fight you every step of the way so that you can't get by with anything shady. I'll keep my share of that company, and I'll persuade my father to put me in charge of it if it's the last thing I do!'

Dane had stopped in the middle of the hall, and he turned to look at her curiously. 'It should be interesting to watch you try,' he said calmly, and walked on.

CHAPTER FIVE

JENNY WRAPPED the crocheted afghan tighter about her and held the book up a little higher so it blocked out the sight of Dane across the living room. He lay on the rug in front of the fireplace, wrestling with Finnegan, who was worrying Dane's foot as if it were a rabbit.

The grandfather clock chimed heavily, and Jenny turned another page. Then she realised that she hadn't the remotest idea what the author was talking about and laid the book aside. 'I hope the brute eats you alive,' she said finally.

Dane sat up. 'You're heartless, Red. At least I don't actively wish you ill.'

She reached for the plate of cookies that sat on the table beside her chair, thoughtfully dipped a chocolate one into her glass of milk, and took a bite.

'Are you already doing research on the products we sell?' Dane asked. 'I can't wait to hear all the wonderful ideas for improving the bakery. Tell me, do you concentrate on the product or do you tackle the whole operation in one bite?'

'I don't intend to confine myself to polling consumers in the supermarkets, if that's what you mean.

Public relations includes a lot of territory, Dane—from tours of the plant on down.'

He sighed. 'That's what I was afraid of. The offer I made this afternoon stands, Red. Forty dollars a share, cash, and all you have to do is leave me alone.'

'What are you trying to hide, Dane?' Jenny asked. 'I'm not so dumb that I can't see through your concern.'

'If you're so wise, you'll figure it out without my help.'

Finnegan, who had sat patiently waiting for the game to be resumed, tugged at Dane's hand, and Jenny shivered at the sight of the big jaw clamping down, almost engulfing Dane's whole hand, but Dane just laughed. 'He never puts any pressure on it,' he pointed out. 'It's a whole new experience in trust to put your hand into the mouth of a dog who could cripple you. You should try it some time.' He reached for a rubber bone. 'Here boy—want to play tug-of-war?'

'Both of you are savages,' Jenny sniffed, and turned back to her book.

'Or would you rather sit quietly and listen to good music, Finnegan? A little Wagner, perhaps?'

Jenny shuddered.

Dane grinned. 'I know—some Ravel would suit the mood right now.'

'If you put ''bolero'' on I'll go spend the evening in the kitchen with Muriel!' Jenny threatened.

Dane rolled to his feet in a single lithe motion. 'If

that's the case, why didn't I think of it long ago?' He headed for the record cabinet.

Jenny slammed her book down on the table, draped the bright afghan across the back of the chair, and left the room as the first quiet strains of the bassoon whispered through the room.

Muriel was humming as she rolled the pastry on the butcher block island in the centre of the kitchen. She looked up with a smile. 'Did you let Dane drive you out?' she asked as Jenny pulled up a stool and sat down with a sigh.

'It was either that or kill him,' Jenny said. 'What are you doing here on a Sunday night, anyway?'

'My husband bowls, so if I want a day off during the week I just come over and whip up some casseroles while he's gone. Tonight I'm working on the Christmas goodies. It takes an awful lot of munchies to keep that Christmas morning crowd happy, and it's only ten days away.'

'Can I help?'

Muriel pushed a bowl of fruit filling across the counter. 'You sure can. Just put a spoonful of this in the middle of each pastry square.'

After the final thunderous repetition of 'Bolero' had died away in the living room, Muriel said, 'Do you miss your young man?'

Jenny looked up in surprise, her spoon suspended in mid-air. 'No. Why?' She hadn't thought of Brian all day, she realised.

'Since he hasn't called you—'

'We aren't engaged, Muriel. And he called last night.'

'Are you going to be engaged?'

'I don't know. I think he'll propose. You'll like him, Muriel.'

Muriel rolled out another ball of dough into an enormous flaky square. She looked thoughtful as she ran the sharp knife through the tender dough. But before she could comment, the telephone rang suddenly.

The strident sound brought fear to Jenny's eyes; Margaret was at the hospital, but any call produced instant concern for Richard. Then she remembered the message Dane had given her last night.

'That's probably Brian now,' she said, and dashed for the phone.

'I'm glad you decided to be around when I called this time, Jennifer,' Brian said.

'I'm sorry I wasn't here last night.'

'Did you have a good time on your date?'

'Yes. You sound angry.'

'I am. I was surprised when Rosemary told me you'd dashed out to the middle of nowhere to hold your sick father's hand, but to call you and find that you're out on a date instead…'

Jenny laughed. 'There isn't a lot of excitement in Twin Rivers, Brian. And no matter what my beloved stepbrother told you, it wasn't really even a date. It was just a group of people going to a play together.' And damn Dane anyway, she thought. Anybody else would have just said she was out, leaving the impression she was at the hospital. Only Dane would go out of his way to cause trouble for her. How he must have enjoyed the opportunity!

'I'm sorry if I sound grouchy, Jennifer, though I must admit I expected you to be at the hospital if you weren't home. I guess I'm just disappointed that my beautiful Jennifer wasn't bored to tears and waiting impatiently for the phone to ring.'

'Since it had been four days since I'd heard from you, I wasn't counting on you calling on Saturday night,' Jenny explained.

'I was out of town. Rosemary didn't catch me with the news till yesterday. Why didn't you call me before you left? That really took me by surprise.'

'I was in too big a hurry.'

'To get home to—what's the name of that place?'

'Twin Rivers. And there's no need to be snide, Brian. It was a good play, even if it is, by your standards, a very small town.' At least half the group had thought it was a good play, she consoled herself.

'How Twin Rivers, Iowa, could discover anything Broadway missed is hard to believe. When will you be home? How's your father doing?'

'Daddy's doing very well. He's out of intensive care, and he'll be home next week. But I'm not coming back for a while.'

There was a silence on the other end of the line. 'You're what?'

'I'm going to stay. At least for the winter.'

'But you can't just go off halfway across the country to stay! A few days is one thing, Jennifer, but to stay for months—you can't do it!'

'Why can't I?' Jenny asked reasonably. 'I've already mailed my resignation. My job is the only commitment I have.'

'What about Rosemary?' asked Brian. 'What does she think?'

'I haven't told her yet. But Brian, she's leaving for the Caribbean in a week and she won't be home till the middle of January. She won't miss me.'

'What about us?'

'Since we're not engaged, I don't think you have a great deal to say about my plans. I'm going to miss you, but I've chosen to stay here for a few months.'

'But Rosemary is expecting to announce our engagement at her next big party, Jennifer. She can't very well do it if you aren't here.'

'I don't think she should plan the engagement party until we've decided to be engaged,' said Jenny coolly.

'Oh, Jennifer, don't be impossible! It's all understood—Rosemary and I talked about it months ago.'

'Isn't it a pity neither of you discussed it with me?'

'Rosemary isn't going to understand this...'

'Yes, she will. You'll do a wonderful job of explaining it to her.'

'Who is he, Jennifer?'

'Who is who?' Jenny was mystified.

'The man you were out with last night. The man who's making you wonder—who's making you question whether you want to marry me. The girl who left here the other night wasn't wondering.'

'Brian, you sound jealous. I refuse to try to defend my behaviour when it doesn't need defending.'

A voice murmured into her other ear. 'I told you he wouldn't like the idea of you dating Steve.' Dane reached over her head to get the corn popper out of the cabinet.

'Would you just shut up?' Jenny hissed.

'Jennifer!' Brian sounded shocked. 'I think it would be a mistake to pursue this conversation any further right now. I'll call you in a couple of days when you've had a chance to cool off. Goodbye.'

Jenny put the phone down with a bang and turned on Dane. 'Well, are you happy now that Brian's mad at me?'

Dane looked thoughtful. 'Should I be? I never considered him to be important in my life.' He bent to look into a low cabinet and she had to strangle the urge to kick him.

From the doorway came a low, soothing voice. 'Dane, honey, let me help. I make terrific popcorn. I know, let's stir up some caramel sauce and make popcorn balls.' Suzanne Sumpter had come in from the living room, slim and elegant in the highest-heeled shoes Jenny had ever seen, paired with tight jeans and a sweater that looked as if she had grown up while she was wearing it.

Jenny muttered, 'And let's have an old-fashioned

taffy pull while we're at it. I want to start with Suzanne's hair!'

Muriel gave her a twisted smile, but addressed Suzanne. 'Sorry, I have so many projects started tonight there isn't room for caramel corn. But if you want to string some popcorn, I'm sure the birds would appreciate the snack.'

Suzanne pouted a little and rubbed her head across Dane's shoulder.

I hope she uses a permanent hair colour, Jenny thought. He's going to look a little odd with one blond shoulder.

'We could go up to the cabin, Dane,' Suzanne said sweetly. 'Then we could do what we wanted to, and we wouldn't get in anybody's way.'

'Sorry, I'm not up to a drive tonight, even just a few miles. Perhaps you hadn't noticed, but it's snowing again. Those gravel roads out there get slick with the smallest of snowfalls.'

Jenny shook her head disapprovingly. 'I'm disappointed in you, Dane.' She perched on her stool beside the butcher block again, her elbows on the countertop.

'But you have the jeep, Dane,' Suzanne said plaintively. 'And it's so nice up there in the evenings, so quiet with no phone or anything.'

'No one to intrude,' Jenny put in helpfully.

Dane glared at her, but before he had a chance to answer, there was a bang at the back door. He stalked across the room and opened it.

Steve peered into the room. 'I thought I smelled Muriel's cooking from down the street,' he said. 'My nose is improving.'

The housekeeper laughed. 'Come on in, scamp. You can fight over the ones that don't come out just right.' She slid a tray of cherry tarts into the oven.

'Best offer I've had all day.' Steve winced and grabbed at his ribs.

'What's the matter?' Jenny was on her feet instantly.

'Nothing much—just your Christmas present scratching me. If you decide you want it, that is.'

'What is it?'

Steve unzipped his jacket and caught a tiny black kitten as it started to tumble out. The little body was almost round, with a stubby tail and a single patch of white on the stomach.

'Oh, let me have him!' Jenny cuddled the kitten close and nuzzled her face into the furry body. 'Where did you get him?'

'My landlady's cat has a litter to give away. He's the only all-black one, though. I thought he was the prettiest, and he's certainly the most active.'

'Fitting gift,' said Suzanne. 'You're obviously too busy to have time for me tonight, Dane. Don't worry about me, I can get my coat. I'll see you tomorrow.' She didn't wait for an answer before she stalked out of the room.

'Poor Suzanne,' Jenny commiserated under her breath.

'What ails Sexy Suzanne?' Steve asked. 'Oops—
that just slipped out, Dane. Sorry.'

'Sexy Suzanne?' Jenny asked. The kitten had discovered that swatting a lock of her hair made it swing,
and he settled in to entertain himself.

'That's what the boys in the back room call her,'
Steve said reluctantly.

'Let's not let it spread to the front room, shall we?'
Dane asked coldly.

'Right,' Steve agreed. If Dane had been looking at
him, Jenny thought, he would probably have saluted.

But Dane was still looking for the popcorn, and
Steve was preoccupied with what he could say to re-
trieve himself. Muriel was concentrating on getting
just the right amount of water into a new batch of
piecrust, and Jenny was trying to disentangle her hair
from the kitten's grasp. Just then Finnegan lumbered
through the swinging door, lonely for all the humans
who until a few minutes ago had been keeping him
company.

The kitten saw Finnegan at the same instant that
Finnegan spotted the unusual furry bundle in Jenny's
arms. The cat hissed and the fur on its back stood
straight up. Then the dog raised up on his haunches
to get a better look, and the kitten took one swipe at
Finnegan's nose before climbing Jenny's throat to escape into an open cupboard door.

Jenny screamed and clutched her throat. The dog
barked twice and then settled down to a steady, gruff
growl. Dane dropped the plastic sack of popcorn,

which split and rattled over the entire floor. Muriel forgot there was a pan on the stove burner and swung around, knocking it off. Only Steve was still, standing in the centre of the room, watching the destruction.

Dane crossed the room to Jenny in two steps, pulling her hand away from the injured throat, where the kitten's claws had drawn streaks of blood. 'It feels horrible!' she wailed. 'Is it that bad?'

'Bad enough. You look like a barber's pole.' He pulled her hair back from the side of her face to expose another long scratch. 'But I don't think it's deep enough to scar.' He glanced over at Steve, who had recovered enough to start trying to talk the kitten down. 'You won't have much luck till you get the dog out, Steve.'

'Stop worrying about that, Dane,' Muriel ordered from the floor where she was wiping up apple pie filling, 'and get something on those scratches of hers.'

'Come on,' Dane ordered Jenny.

'I can get it on by myself.'

'No, you can't, not unless you can see behind your left ear.' He pulled her down the hall to the small, elegant powder room and searched through the medicine cabinet. 'Sit down,' he ordered, pointing to the edge of the sink.

'Margaret will kill me if I bleed in here,' she protested.

'If we're lucky she'll never know anything about it.' He picked her up and set her on the sink. 'Take a deep breath—this will sting.'

It did. The scratches were long and deep, and each gentle stroke of the cotton wool swab brought fresh tears to Jenny's eyes.

'What are you going to name the cat?' Dane asked.

Jenny looked up, startled. 'How did you know I'm going to keep it?'

'It just seems the sort of convoluted, idiotic thing you'd do. Can I suggest a name?'

'I don't promise to use it,' she said warily.

'Lucifer. If there ever was an imp of Satan, that kitten is it.'

Jenny sat up straight. 'And just what does that mean? The cat was fine till Finnegan poked his nose in. That dog is trouble with a capital T.'

'He was only being curious,' Dane explained.

'And if something fifty times your size came pounding up to you, wouldn't you be a little nervous, too?'

'A little nervous? You should see yourself. It's too bad Hallowe'en is past; you could have gone to the masquerade party as a pinstriped suit.'

'Will it scar, Dane? Truth!' she begged.

'You might look as if you've had an early facelift.' He saw her tears start again and relented. 'No, it won't scar, Red. It was only a little kitten.' He put the antiseptic bottle back on the shelf. 'That should do it. Now I need two things. The first is your promise that as soon as Lucifer teaches Finnegan to leave him alone, you'll get the cat de-clawed.'

'I suppose that's the only practical way,' Jenny said reluctantly.

'You'd better believe it. If you think Mother would kill you for bleeding in her fancy powder room, wait till you see what she does the first time the cat sharpens its claws on her favourite chair!'

'I see your point. And the second thing?'

'Hmm. On second thought, I think I'll collect my thank-you later. I never did like kissing girls who'd been crying. Off you go.'

JENNY CLOSED THE FILE that lay on her desk blotter and picked up her coffee cup, cradling it between her hands as she thought about the information she had been trying to absorb. There was nothing wrong with the annual sales figures, she knew, in fact, sales and profits had been well above the previous year's mark. But there was something that she couldn't quite put her finger on—something that could make all the difference to Twin Rivers Bakeries if she could only see what it was.

She sipped and made a face. If there was one thing she couldn't stand, it was cold coffee. She wondered idly if Suzanne had put an ice cube in the cup before she had brought it in. Suzanne wasn't above it, she had made Jenny's first days in the office difficult. She was never openly hostile and she always did what Jenny asked her to do, but she did it very slowly.

Jenny wondered if Dane had actually instructed Suzanne to make things difficult for her, or if it was

Suzanne's own idea. Probably Dane knew nothing about it. Jenny knew she had been catty on Sunday when Suzanne had been at the house, and she was being paid back for it in kind.

Or perhaps Suzanne was just subtly letting Jenny know that she considered Dane to be her private property no matter where he was. She certainly never missed a chance to be close to him—leaning over his shoulder, brushing a fleck off his shirt, giving him a sultry smile.

'Little does she know she has nothing to fear from me,' said Jenny. She picked up her cup and started for the coffee room, thinking what a pity it was that Dane refused to wear a tie. If he would acquire that habit, she thought sarcastically, he'd never need to straighten it himself!

The radio on a high shelf in the coffee room was blaring Country and Western music, and beneath a speaker, Steve and Jim were sitting, a tray of fresh doughnuts between them, drinking black coffee.

'How can you stand that?' asked Jenny, refilling her cup.

'Stand what?' Steve asked dryly. 'The music, the noise level, or the food staring us in the face?'

'Specifically, the noise level.'

'It grows on you. Have a chair.'

'Only if you aren't talking about anything important.'

'We weren't even talking,' said Jim. 'It was more like shouting.'

'I'm surprised Dane allows anything but classical music,' Jenny remarked.

'Oh, Dane's a pretty tolerant guy, most of the time.' Jim got up and stood on his chair to reach the control knobs on the radio. 'How's that?'

'Better—but if you could find some Rachmaninoff I'd like it even more,' said Steve.

'Not you too? Do you realise,' Jenny said soberly, 'that fully half the people who work here would think you'd just asked for a new brand of cheese?'

Jim climbed down off his chair. 'You mean it isn't?' he teased. 'And I was getting all ready to go out for crackers!'

'You are crackers, Jim.' Jenny retorted. 'How do you guys sit here with all this food and just ignore it?'

'Believe me, doughnuts get to looking mighty dull after a few years around this place,' said Jim.

'I guess I'll have to let the attraction wear off.' Jenny chose an enormous glazed doughnut and bit into it. 'I just got a terrific idea for a new ad,' she said. 'There's this little tiny kid with this gigantic doughnut, see, and he bites into it and says…' She took another bite. 'I'll have to think about it some more.'

'Have another doughnut while you think,' Jim advised, pushing the tray a little closer. 'How's it going after three days?'

'Oh, I'm surviving. The fact that Dane hasn't been here much has helped, I'm sure.'

'That cabin of his is nice, but I didn't think it was that attractive,' Jim mused.

'Oh, he's been around. He's just been hiding out in the lab. He must have a new project started.' Steve sipped his coffee. 'Wonder what it is this time.'

'It could be anything from perfume to weedkiller. One never knows with Dane.' Jim got up to refill his cup.

'What lab?' asked Jenny.

'Didn't you know he's fitted up one of the little back rooms as a chemistry lab?' Steve asked.

'So that's where he spends all his time,' she mused, wondering if her father knew about this. 'Playing with noxious mixtures and waiting for something to explode.'

Jim looked unhappy. 'Jen, a lot of his stuff has practical applications. Last summer he developed a new blend of oils to grease the bread pans...'

'Have you ever been inside his lab?'

Jim looked shocked. 'Inside Dane's private lab? Are you kidding?'

'Then how do you know what goes on there?'

'It certainly isn't orgies, if that's what you're thinking.'

Steve tried to sidetrack the argument. 'Have you decided to go to the company Christmas party on Saturday night, Jenny?'

'I hadn't thought about it. But I suppose I should go.'

'I thought perhaps Dane was taking you.'

'Dane?' Jenny's tone was shocked. 'Why would he want to take me? He's refusing to admit I even work here. No, he hasn't said a word, and he won't. Dane doesn't want to spend a whole evening with me, any more than I want to spend one with him.'

'Just what do you have against Dane, anyway?' Jim asked curiously. 'He's one of the nicest guys I know.'

'Obviously you don't know too many,' Jenny retorted.

'In that case, would you like to go with me?' asked Steve, ignoring the byplay. 'It's always a nice party— terrific food and a dance afterwards.'

'Where is it?' asked Jenny.

'Out at the Lemon Tree.'

'Where's that?'

'It's new since you left, Jenny,' Jim explained. 'It's one of the old houses out by the Country Club. They remodelled and built on banquet facilities. You'll like it. Why don't you two go with Alison and me?'

'Go where with us, Jim?'

Jim turned to look over his shoulder. 'Speak of the devil,' he said as Alison came across the room, the baby on her hip. 'To the Christmas party on Saturday.'

Jenny reached for Molly, who held up fat little arms encased in pink fur. She settled the infant on her lap and unzipped her snowsuit. Molly giggled and blew a saliva bubble.

'Watch out or she'll spit up all over that gorgeous jacket,' Alison warned. 'She just ate her afternoon snack. Here, you'd better have a spare diaper.' She pulled one out of her bag and handed it to Jenny.

'I won't fall apart if she acts like a baby, Alison,' Jenny protested.

'You might not, but I probably would. That outfit must have cost you a fortune. Are you coming to the party?'

'I don't suppose I dare miss it, and I might as well be in company I enjoy,' said Jenny. 'Of course.'

'I just hope Dane doesn't get upset with me,' Steve muttered.

'Why would he? He doesn't want me around, I told you. Besides, he's probably taking Suzanne.'

'Yes, he is.' Alison poured herself a cup of coffee and sat down next to Jim. 'She just told me all about it when I called in to her office to see where everybody was.'

Molly decided abruptly that she wanted her mother and strained to get out of Jenny's arms.

'And I wonder why I need a break from this child,' Alison groaned as she reached for Molly. 'Can we go to Chicago the weekend after Christmas, Jim? I'm dying to see the decorations on State Street.'

'If you can find a babysitter, dear. And the money. I wish you luck on both counts at this season of the year,' Jim warned.

'I'll babysit, Alison,' offered Jenny.

'You're an angel, Jen. But I wouldn't ask that of anybody who's holding down a full-time job. Jim, I came round to get the chequebook, and then I'll leave you all alone.' She zipped up Molly's snowsuit.

Jim groaned. 'I won't ever see it again, I suppose,' he growled, pulling the chequebook out of his hip pocket.

Alison smiled. 'Of course you'll get it back. The very next time it needs to be balanced, I promise.' She tucked the book into her bag, and picked Molly up.

'Just a minute, Alison,' said Jenny, draining her coffee cup. 'I'll grab my coat and walk out to the parking lot with you. I'm ready to leave.'

Suzanne looked up with a smile as they came into the office, but the expression died quickly when she realised that it wasn't Dane standing there.

'I'm going up to the hospital and then home, in case anyone is looking for me,' said Jenny, and went on into her office to clear her desk and get her coat. She thought she heard Suzanne mutter something about privileged employees and bankers' hours, but she ignored it.

When she came back out, Dane was leaning over Suzanne's chair, and the secretary was pointing out a line in the letter she was typing. He wore a long white coat and his hair was rumpled; he had obviously been called out of his lab. One brown hand was braced on Suzanne's desk; as Jenny watched the secretary's fingers crept closer and closer.

Jenny fumed, can't they at least keep their attraction for each other away from the office? 'Well, Dane, so you finally found your way to work,' she commented. 'After all, it is only four in the afternoon.'

'Hello, Red. Are you leaving already?' Dane settled himself on the edge of Suzanne's desk and folded his arms across his broad chest. No wonder Suzanne had wanted to be alone with him over the weekend, Jenny thought. Even with his hair rumpled, he exuded a masculine super-confidence that was disturbing to the female of the species. Not in the least exciting, she told herself, but definitely disturbing.

'I've been here since eight this morning,' she said.

'Believe it or not, so have I.'

'But not engaged in bakery business.'

'You seem very certain of that.' Dane's eyes roamed over her. 'How are your scratches doing?' He lifted a hand to brush her hair back from the side of her face, to inspect the skin where Lucifer's claws had struck.

Jenny pulled away. 'Just fine, thank you.'

'You'd better let me look. Who knows if that cat was clean. You don't want them to get infected.'

She sighed and let him lift the lock of hair. If Dane was determined to inspect those scratches, he'd go to any lengths to do so, and she might as well stop arguing.

He studied the scratch, then pulled her deeply-rolled collar away from her throat so he could see the rest of the damage. With a gentle finger he traced each of the four parallel scratches, smiling grimly as Jenny shuddered under his hand.

'They're healing nicely,' he said at last. 'Just don't disturb them, and you won't even have a mark to show where they were.' His hand slipped to the nape of her neck and lay warm against her skin as he massaged the muscles.

'Thank you, Dr Sutherland,' Jenny said sarcastically, and pointedly removed his hand from inside her collar.

'They were into it again when I was home for lunch,' Dane reported. 'Lucifer was playing with one of Mother's plants, and Finnegan knew he shouldn't be. I'm afraid my dog is going to have a nervous breakdown because of your cat.'

'I doubt it. There has to be a certain amount of intelligence present for there to be mental illness, and I don't think Finnegan has it in him.'

'Sibling rivalry is terrible, isn't it!' Dane drawled.

As Jenny turned towards Alison, who had been waiting patiently in a chair near the door, she caught a glimpse of cold anger gleaming in Suzanne's eyes. She had an enemy there, no doubt of it.

'I'm parked out in the employee's lot,' said Alison. 'Shall we cut through the bakery and save ourselves from the cold?'

The day's work was winding down as the last of the golden-brown loaves of bread circled high above their heads, cooling as they travelled along the precisely-timed endless conveyer. The ovens had shut down for the day, but the last loaves were making their meandering way towards the slicing and sacking machines. The aroma of fresh-baked bread hung like a cloud in the room, pleasantly warm now for the shirt-sleeved workers. In the summer it sometimes reached well above a hundred degrees on the bakery floor.

The clean-up crews were working now on the bread floor, but from above her head Jenny could hear the distinctive rumble of the mixers as they churned out another batch of cookie dough. Cookies were their main product, and that line never stopped.

The cold wind struck the girls full in the face as they stepped out of the employees' entrance. It was a shock after the warmth of the bakery floor.

Alison tucked the blanket closer around Molly's head. 'Brr, it's awfully cold for this early in the winter,' she said. 'I can't wait to find out what it will be like in February. If it keeps up like this I'll have to start chipping myself out of bed in the mornings! Jim said you're staying in Twin Rivers?'

'For the winter.' Jenny changed the subject, not wanting Alison to pursue it. 'What are you wearing to the Christmas party?'

'I have an elegant new dress. I thought the world owed it to me; last Christmas I looked like a water buffalo and I had just about as much grace. It's a disco dance, you know.'

'That sounds like Dane. He probably paid more for the band than for the food, and certainly he chose the music with more care than the menu.'

'Oh, Jenny, I wish you'd stop it!' said Alison.

'Alison, why is everyone around here so blind? Can't you all see what he's doing? He's not running this business; he's cooped up in his precious laboratory all the time, off in his own little world.'

'You've been working here three days and you know it all, is that it, Jenny? It may look to you as if Dane isn't paying any attention, but just wait till something goes wrong and you'll find out that he's the first one to know about it.' Alison strapped Molly into her car seat. 'And let me tell you, Jenny, it's uncomfortable, being Dane's friend and listening to you. I love you, but would you just lay off Dane?'

'I don't think I can.'

'Give it your best shot,' retorted Alison, and got into her car.

CHAPTER SIX

CHASTENED BY Alison's angry accusations, Jenny drove slowly up to the hospital on the hill. Was her friend right? Dane had a great deal of charm when he chose to use it, and apparently he had chosen to display it to Alison. That was all it was, Jenny told herself. At least she herself wasn't so blind.

Richard had been waiting for her, for as soon as she appeared in his room his face lighted up, and he tossed his magazine down on the table beside his chair.

Jenny shed her coat and draped it over a chair. 'Interesting reading you're doing,' she observed. The *National Geographic* he had put down was twelve years old.

'And not only old, but they cut all the pictures of the natives out so we heart patients wouldn't get too excited,' Richard mourned. 'Is that a new outfit?'

Jenny pirouetted, showing off the velvet blazer and blue plaid skirt. 'Yes—purchased on credit till I get my first pay-cheque. I assume this job does include payday, even if I did sort of hire myself?'

'Oh, yes—eventually. What's going on at home?'

'We put up the Christmas tree last night, and Lucifer climbed it. Actually, Finnegan chased him up it.'

'That's an event I'm delighted to have missed,' said Richard dryly.

'You always hated trimming the tree, didn't you, Daddy? What kind of Scrooge are you, anyway? It's a beautiful Norwegian pine. Dane brought it in from the country, and he does know how to pick a tree.'

'I'm glad he can do something to suit you. I was beginning to wonder.'

Jenny frowned at him, but didn't answer. 'And Aunt Agnes called. She'll be here this weekend and she'll stay till the holidays are over.'

'Oh, my beloved sister! Perhaps I don't want to come home after all.' His forehead was wrinkled in thought. 'Did you buy my Christmas gift for Margaret?'

'I certainly did. I think you'll like it. And I know she'll like it, but I warn you, it cost an arm and a leg.' She reached into her handbag.

'I knew it would be expensive when I told you to buy something you'd like to have for yourself,' Richard teased.

Jenny put her hands on her hips and frowned at him. 'You're the one who taught me to appreciate the best, Daddy,' she pointed out. She tossed a box at him. 'Now name a woman who wouldn't like to find that under the Christmas tree!'

He caught the box and slid the cover off. Winking up at him from the dark green velvet was a diamond dinner ring, a magnificent cluster of stones surrounding a single large emerald. He whistled. 'An arm and *both* legs, don't you mean, Jennifer?' he asked.

'It was on sale,' she said practically. 'And Margaret bought a new emerald green dress to wear on Christmas Day. I couldn't resist.' She pulled the ring from the case and slid it on to her own slender finger, turning her hand to admire the sparks that flew from the light fractured by the gems.

'Getting anxious to have a diamond of your own on that finger?' her father asked. 'How's the boyfriend?'

'Mad at me. He hasn't called since Sunday. He doesn't like the idea of me staying. And I don't think I'm in any hurry to be married, anyway.'

'That's good. I'd like to keep you around a while. How is the job going?' asked Richard, stretching his legs out more comfortably.

'Oh, I have such a lot of good ideas! Why haven't arrangements been made to take tour groups through? And there are so many new product areas we could go into. Did you ever think about marketing frozen dough that the housewife just puts in the oven? A lot of companies are doing it and we could too. And I think we should...'

'Whoa!' Richard laughed, holding up a hand to protect himself from the onslaught of words. 'Jenny, I'm an old man; I can't take all of this in at once. Besides, it isn't me you need to talk to, dear—it's Dane.'

Jenny gritted her teeth. 'Dane won't listen to a word I say.'

Richard leaned back in his chair and thoughtfully scratched his chin. 'Well, it's only been three days,' he said finally. 'You tend to take a subject by storm, Jen. Give the boy a chance to get used to the idea. Did he say he wouldn't do it, or did he say he'd think about it?'

Jenny fidgeted a minute, then said, 'I haven't actually asked him.'

'Some businesswoman you are!' said Richard, his voice teasingly affectionate.

She flared, 'There hasn't been a chance. He's only been in the building about three hours all week. And half of that time he spent back in his little cubbyhole that I just discovered is fitted up as a chemistry lab. No doubt he was trying to blow the place up.' She eyed her father, wondering if he would be upset at this evidence of Dane's lack of interest in the business.

'Of course it's a lab,' said Richard startled by the question. 'He did that a year ago.'

'Oh, well, if he's doing such a terrible job of managing the bakery, why do you keep him there?'

'Because he isn't doing a terrible job. He's an exceptionally good manager, and he knows how to get the most out of his people.' Richard's eyes were keen on Jenny's face. 'Dane is incapable of doing anything badly; you know that, Jenny. If he's going to do it at all, he does it well.'

'I know. It's one of the most frustrating things about him,' she grumbled. She remembered when Dane had taught her to ski. It was a skill that had come easily to him, but she had struggled to acquire the slightest degree of proficiency.

'You're smart enough that I'll bet you've already seen the balance sheets. What's the problem, Jenny?' His voice was soothing, and she dropped to her knees beside his chair and buried her face in the shoulder of his quilted robe. He stroked the soft red hair. 'Jenny, are you just being a dog in the manger?'

There was an exclamation from the doorway. '*That's* what she reminds me of,' said Dane as he came in. He had left the lab coat at the bakery and looked as if he had just come in from the woods. For all she knew, Jenny reminded herself, he had. Just because he said he had spent the day in the bakery it didn't mean that he had. Nobody had seen much of him, that was sure.

'What do I remind you of?' Jenny asked bitterly, her head still on Richard's shoulder.

Dane settled himself comfortably in the extra chair, stretched his legs out and inspected a scratch on the surface of his leather boot. Finally he looked up. 'Finnegan,' he said.

'The dog?' she asked blankly.

'Yes. You're the same colour.' He reached out and picked up a lock of red-gold hair from where it lay across her shoulder. 'Exactly the same shade. I'm positive of it.' He let the lock of hair drop back against the dark blue velvet collar, and said sweetly, 'It looks as if you could use a good brushing today, too.'

'You'd better watch out. I might decide to bite, like Finnegan does.' Jenny stood up and shook her hair back over her shoulders. 'I'll come back another time, Daddy, when we can talk.'

'Why don't you use this opportunity to tell Dane about your new ideas for the bakery, Jenny? He looks very comfortable; I doubt he'll walk out on you.' Though her father's words were a suggestion, Jenny recognised the order in the tone of his voice.

She sighed and sat down on the edge of the bed, slim fingers pleating the blue bedspread. Her big brown eyes were pleading as she looked up at Dane through long dark lashes. He merely raised an eyebrow, unmoved by her appeal, and she turned back to her father to address her plea.

'I think we should consider major changes in the public relations campaigns. The image of the bakery is of an old-fashioned, dowdy operation. Even the names of the products are old-fashioned and dull as dishwater. We need a new image, some excitement about the products.'

Dane tapped his fingers idly on the arm of his chair. 'I thought you didn't even like the new company name. Now you want to change everything!'

There was no doubt in Jenny's mind where that information had come from. Somehow he had got it out of Steve. But she kept her temper with an effort.

'You're changing the subject, Dane. The company name has nothing to do with making the products more interesting. And some new products wouldn't hurt, either.'

Dane looked bored.

She turned back to Richard. 'We could create a dry mix that would have a better shelf life than the cookies and baked goods do. A lot of the mixes that are on the market now taste just like the cardboard box...'

'That's because they're packed in one,' Dane inserted lazily.

'So we figure out a new package. Why not? Why don't you turn that terrific brain to figuring out how to make a cookie mix that tastes like homemade?'

'Because I'm a chemist, not a short-order cook.'

Jenny sniffed. 'If you don't want to bother working that problem out, how about frozen dough? The woman of the house takes it home and bakes it and nobody knows that she didn't mix it up herself. If all the other companies can do it, we should be able to, with very little increase in overheads. We can put the afternoon shifts to better use that way.'

'Storage,' said Dane.

'What?'

'You haven't considered the problems of storing and shipping frozen dough.'

Jenny looked at her father. 'He's right, Jenny,' Richard agreed calmly.

Jenny merely raised her eyebrows and shrugged.

What's the use? her look said, but she tried one more time. 'I'm sure you could work the problem out if you wanted to,' she said. 'After all, everyone is convinced you're a genius when it comes to chemistry.'

'That's not chemistry either, Red. That is product engineering. And plain common sense says that we can't keep a supply of frozen dough in stock unless we have freezers to store it in and refrigerated trailers to ship it. It would have to be shipped separately from the bread and cookies because they age faster in refrigerated conditions. To say nothing whether the public would buy it.'

'If it was good enough, they would,' Jenny said defiantly.

'Then start by coming up with a recipe and have Muriel try it out.'

'That reminds me—the test kitchens need to be replaced. And a new ad campaign—we definitely need that. The one we're using now is a shambles.'

Dane yawned.

Jenny could have thrown something at him. Instead, she rose, gathering all her dignity. 'Obviously, there's no point in attempting to discuss this,' she told Richard. 'I'll stop by this evening, Daddy, and perhaps we can have a civilised conversation.' She put a kiss on his cheek.

Richard handed her the box for Margaret's ring. 'Don't forget to take off your little treasure before you get home so Margaret doesn't see it,' he advised.

Jenny glanced at the gleam of diamonds on her finger. 'I won't lose it, Daddy.'

'I'll see you tonight, love. Are you going too, Dane?' Richard sounded surprised.

Dane had got to his feet. 'I only came by to beg a ride home with Red,' he said. 'I just left my car up the street to have the oil changed, and I can't pick it up till tomorrow.'

Jenny made a face. 'You're certainly willing enough to accept my help when it suits you!'

'You're learning, Red. Congratulations.'

They were silent as they walked down to Jenny's car. Then she asked, 'Why aren't you willing to listen to any ideas I have, Dane?'

He looked surprised. 'I wasn't aware you were addressing them to me. It looked as if you were talking to your father.'

'You're impossible! Nothing that I come up with will ever be acceptable to you, will it?'

He reached for her car keys and unlocked the passenger door of her car, holding it open for her. Jenny ignored him and held her hand out for the keys. He shrugged and got into the car.

'I don't think I'm impossible,' he countered when she slid beneath the wheel. 'In fact, you might find me quite persuadable if you wanted to work at it.'

'I'd rather kiss a boa constrictor!'

'Oh, I wasn't planning to stop with a kiss this time, Red.'

She decided abruptly that she was tired of playing

games with him, and she came directly to the point. 'Just what is it you want from me, Dane?'

He was equally frank. 'Your shares of stock in Twin Rivers Bakeries. I've always had an urge to own it; I'm sure that comes as no surprise to you.'

'No, I'd managed to guess that. You won't get those shares away from me, Dane. I'd die first—and if I do I'll leave them to…charity, if I have to. Or to the lucky hundredth person to sign the visitors' book at my funeral. Anything to keep them away from you.'

He ignored her outburst. 'I'll offer you fifty a share, by the way, Red. Take it or leave it. You can have the money in time to spend Christmas in the Caribbean, and that's no small matter considering that it's only a week away.'

Jenny shrugged. 'Sorry. It looks to me as if I've earned ten dollars a share since you made that offer on Sunday. I think I'll wait a few days. It will be interesting to see how high you go in a hopeless cause.' She parked the car next to the back door. 'Would you like to tell me where all the money is coming from, by the way?'

'Of course not. That's strictly my business. But be assured that I'm not bluffing. I play fair—'

'Ha!' she interrupted.

'So I'm honour bound to tell you that if you agree to sell me those shares, thinking that you'll humiliate me when I can't come up with the cash, you'll have lost your bet.'

'I think you're bluffing.'

'I hope you don't play much poker, honey. You're not only a naïve player, but you're a bad loser. That offer, by the way, has a time limit on it. Midnight Saturday it expires. Don't try to hold me up the way you're conning Richard.'

'Just what does that mean?' Jenny flared.

Dane picked up her hand. 'Nice little piece of rock you're wearing. A bribe to keep you here? I hope you're worth what you're costing him.'

If he thought she had bought it for herself, Jenny wasn't going to waste her time explaining. 'Why don't you ask him?' she said tightly and slammed the door of the car when she got out.

THE BAND WAS already playing when the foursome left the banqueting room for the dance floor. The Lemon Tree was a spacious nightclub, and tonight both a party room in the restaurant and the big dance floor had been reserved for the employees of the bakery to have their Christmas party.

The toe of Jenny's high-heeled shoe started to tap as soon as she heard the music, and she tugged at Steve's arm. 'Let's dance,' she said.

He groaned. 'Not right now, Jenny. The smorgasbord was so good that I ate enough to feed darkest Africa, and I couldn't dance now if somebody pointed a gun at me!' He pulled out a chair and coaxed her to sit down, his hand trailing across the nape of her neck under the upswept hair.

Jim shook his head at Alison. 'Same goes for me, honey. And by the way, why don't you ever cook a meal like that for me?'

'Because if I did you'd weigh four hundred pounds by next Christmas,' Alison retorted.

She sat down beside Jenny, who said, 'We could go dance together, Alison. This is worse than it was in high school when we didn't have dates and the boys didn't want to dance.'

'How would you know?' Alison retorted. 'There was never a high school dance you didn't have a date for.' Her face brightened. 'There's Dane—he'll dance. He's the only man I know who really likes to.'

Jenny glanced around warily, hoping to spot Dane without drawing his attention to her. He was across the room, dressed as formally as she had ever seen him, in a dark brown sports jacket and beige trousers. His cream-coloured shirt was open at the collar, however. Suzanne had apparently won the skirmish but lost the war; not even all the persuasion that Jenny had been overhearing all week had persuaded him to put on a tie.

Jenny smiled a secret little smile—so Suzanne wasn't having as much luck with him as she liked to pretend!—and turned back to Alison. 'Didn't you see Suzanne hanging on his arm?'

The little brunette looked disgruntled. 'That kills all hope. She'll monopolise him all evening.'

'It does seem only fair,' Jenny said mildly.

'What's fair about it? Are you back to the assumption that he's planning to marry her?'

'He's spending all his time with her.'

Jim leaned forward. 'Dane has a lot more sense than that,' he said flatly.

'Sorry, Jim, I have trouble believing as you do.'

Alison sighed. 'Jenny!' she said warningly.

'All right, I'll quit talking about Dane. I know it makes you angry when I say anything about your charming little friend.'

'I can't imagine you being quiet on the subject of Dane. I just wish you'd make an effort to understand him a little better. He's an extremely sensitive person...'

Jenny made a sound that might have been called a snort. 'Dane is almost as sensitive as a barbed-wire fence!'

Alison ignored her. 'His father was just plain mean, Jenny. Any other kid would have believed it when his father pounded into him that he was no good. But Dane ended up better for it—surer of himself, understanding of others.'

Jenny raised an eyebrow. 'Oh, really?'

Alison went on. 'I think you were hurt the same way by your mother, Jen. And you think that makes it all right for you to be cold and cynical, because you've been hurt. But you aren't willing to give Dane the time of day—you think it's wrong if the hurt he suffered still comes back to him sometimes.'

'Alison, shush!' Jim put in firmly.

'That's quite all right, Jim,' Jenny said blandly. 'What are friends for?'

'There! That's exactly the attitude I was talking about when I said you're cold and cynical,' Alison pointed out. 'And to answer the question, friends are there to tell you what you can't see for yourself.'

Jim took Alison's arm and pulled her to her feet. 'We're going to go dance,' he announced before she could say anything more.

Steve sipped his drink and finally broke the silence. 'Are you mad at Alison?'

'You might say that,' Jenny agreed.

'What did Dane do to you, anyway?' Then he caught himself. 'Sorry, it's none of my business. How is the kitten doing?'

'Oh, he's in heaven. He thinks we decorated the Christmas tree just for him—he knocks bulbs off it and chases them around the floor. He broke three last night. Margaret scolds him and Lucifer just sits down with his back to her and washes himself. It drives her nuts. Let's go and dance.'

They brushed against Suzanne and Dane on the dance floor once. The blonde girl gave Jenny a smug smile and snuggled a little closer into Dane's broad shoulder. It was a slow number, and Jenny put her head down on Steve's shoulder and closed her eyes. It was no problem to ignore them, she found, as long as she couldn't see them. The only problem was that Steve was a really bad dancer.

Alison and Jim were already at the table when they

came back, and Alison looked worried. Jenny had scarcely sat down when she leaned across the table and said, 'I shouldn't have said that, Jenny. Can we just forget that I opened my big mouth?'

Jenny studied her for a minute and then nodded. 'Friends?'

'Friends.' The word was a sigh of relief. Alison reached across the table to squeeze Jenny's hand. 'I'm glad I didn't ruin everything.'

But there was a strained silence for a few minutes. Then Steve asked idly, 'Are you going to Chicago after Christmas?'

'No, worse luck,' Alison mourned. 'I've always wanted to see State Street decorated for Christmas, and I won't get to do it this year either.'

'Couldn't you find a sitter? I'll keep Molly if I can come over to your house,' Jenny offered. 'Now that Daddy's home I don't think he'd appreciate a baby in the house the first weekend, especially right after all the excitement of Christmas.'

'Oh, I didn't even try too hard. Jim says we can't afford to go anywhere, but I think we need a little time to ourselves.'

Jim looked up in surprise. 'Didn't I tell you Dane said we could have his cabin next weekend?'

'You certainly didn't.' Alison turned to Jenny. 'You haven't been up there, have you? It's so pretty up there in the summer with the quiet and the trees and the little creek...'

'And the mosquitoes,' Steve added dryly, and signalled the waitress.

'You just don't appreciate the joys of country living, Steve.'

'You'll freeze up there in the middle of winter.'

'No, we won't,' Jim countered. 'That's why I'm taking Alison. She can chop wood and keep the fires going and cook farmhand meals for me...'

'If you're going to be doing all that, it sounds as if you'll need a babysitter. You won't have time to take care of Molly, that's for sure.' Jenny stirred the ice in her glass and shook her head at the waitress.

'It does sound good. If you're sure, Jenny...'

'Positive. I'll take the baby and you go have fun communing with nature and remembering why you got married.'

'How is your dad feeling now that he's home?' Jim asked.

'He's just as unmanageable as ever. He announced that he was going to make an appearance at the party tonight, but Margaret vetoed it. I think he was secretly happy she did, because it's so cold and he tires very quickly. After all, he's only been home for a day and a half. He's hardly in any shape to run a marathon, but you'd never get him to admit it.'

'I was surprised when Dane said he was going to officially retire. But I'm sure the second heart attack in a couple of years would make you think about it.'

'I'm just glad he can be home for Christmas.

Daddy's such a sentimental soul that I don't think he could bear an institutional holiday,' said Jenny.

'Are you going to have the usual big event?' Alison asked.

'On a smaller scale, I think. I don't know just how big it's been the last few years. But Aunt Agnes is coming. I just hope she won't insist on arguing with him.'

'Where has she been this time?'

'Who knows? Singapore, I think. Or perhaps it was Tibet. But everyone will know by the time she leaves.'

The dance band started to play a slow number, and Steve reached for Jenny's hand. 'Now this is my kind of music,' he said. 'Let's dance, Jenny.'

She had to force herself to relax, and she was just starting to enjoy herself when Steve stopped abruptly in the middle of the floor. She opened her eyes, startled to see Dane looking down at her. 'Sorry, Steve,' he was saying, 'but I haven't had a chance to talk to Jenny all evening.'

'Just give her back in one piece, Dane,' Steve joked, and went back to the table.

'No, thanks,' said Jenny, and started to follow him, but somehow she found herself in Dane's arms in the middle of the dance floor instead. It would have been impossible to break free without creating a scene, even if she had the physical strength to do so. So she stared at the lapels of his corduroy jacket and tried to forget where she was.

'No, thanks, what?' he asked smoothly.

'I don't want to dance with you.'

'I can't say that this is the highlight of my evening, either, but I'm sure you know some new steps that I want to learn.'

'That doesn't mean you have to learn them from me.'

'And who else around here knows them? You're a poor sport, Red. Remember who taught you to dance in the first place?'

'All right, I owe you. Why did you devote so much time to tutoring me, anyway?'

'It was the only way I could…' Dane stopped suddenly and Jenny had the impression that he had swallowed whatever it was that he had intended to say. 'It was the one way to keep you from throwing things at me,' he amended. 'As long as you were dancing, you were too busy.'

'Pay close attention now,' Jenny directed.

Dane mimicked her steps effortlessly, picking up the subtle rhythms of a dance it had taken her a week to learn. 'You didn't look comfortable dancing with Steve. Was it Steve, or were you thinking about what's-his-name?'

'His name, if you must use it, is Brian. Remember?'

'Ah, yes. How could I forget? Are you ice-cold with him too, or is it just Steve? I know it isn't all men—you certainly have proved to me that you aren't frigid.'

Jenny stumbled, and Dane held her even closer. 'Sorry, Jenny. Did I trip you?' he asked solicitously.

'You're an animal, Dane Sutherland!' she snapped.

'I knew we'd get back to that some day. As a matter of fact, I am. But then so are you, Red—a very hot-blooded animal. Would you like me to take you off in a secluded corner and prove it to you?'

Jenny broke free. 'Just leave me alone, Dane. That's the only thing I ask.' She stalked across the room towards her table.

He caught up with her halfway across the dance floor. 'Oh, I think you're asking for a lot more than that, Jenny,' he said silkily. 'Watch out, darling, because you're apt to get what you're looking for.'

'You two really look good dancing together, Jenny,' said Alison. 'I just wish… No, don't glare at me, please. I'll be quiet. Who's that, Jim?' She flicked a glance towards the door.

'I don't know him. He doesn't belong to the bakery, does he, Steve?'

'I don't think he belongs in Twin Rivers. There can't be more than six men in this town who own dinner jackets, and it looks like he lives in his.'

Jenny choked on her ice cube and swung around in her chair. 'Brian!' she breathed, not believing her own eyes.

Brian Randall stood in the doorway of the ballroom, his steady gaze flicking over the tables as he searched for her. The room seemed to waver around her, and then suddenly she was running across the room to greet him. She flung herself into his arms and he bent his head to kiss her cheek.

'So you have missed me after all,' he said smiling. 'I must say I'm not surprised. Do you know how difficult it is to make connections to get here? And renting a car is a real trial. Neither Hertz nor Avis has ever heard of Twin Rivers, Iowa, and they rebel at renting cars to go places they never knew existed.'

'Oh, Brian, I have missed you! I didn't know how much till you walked in.'

His eyes rested on the table she had risen from. 'I can't believe that,' he said, with a hint of sarcasm. 'We're making a scene, Jennifer. All the yokels are staring. Shall we dance?'

She went willingly into his arms, her cheek against his shoulder. 'How did you find me?' she asked.

'I finally stumbled across your house, and your stepmother directed me here. She told me it was a party—some party, I should think. Such sartorial elegance!'

'Oh, it's the Christmas affair for the employees of the bakery,' Jenny explained.

Brian closed his eyes briefly as though in pain. 'Ah, yes, I should have guessed.'

'Why are you here?' she wanted to know.

'I wanted to see you. And Rosemary asked me to come. She thinks you've lost your mind, and she wants me to bring you back. She has the best psychiatrist in the state with a couch on hold for you.'

Jenny giggled. 'I'm not insane, Brian.'

'Good. Then you'll come back with me.'

'No. I'm staying the winter.'

'Very well.'

She peeped up at him through narrowed eyes. 'Do you mean you're giving up so easily?'

'Oh, no, I just don't believe in fighting in public. We'll take up the subject of your irrational thinking later. That's a nice scent you're wearing, by the way. A new one?'

'I don't think so. Margaret loaned it to me.'

'And Margaret is…?'

'My stepmother. Did she give you a room at the house?'

'Yes. I think I'll like her, Jennifer. I was my most charming, of course, and she reacted very well.'

Jenny felt an uncomfortable twinge at his words. Brian's charm was one of his greatest assets, but sometimes it seemed to her that he was too deliberate with its use. But she thrust the idea way. Of course he wanted Margaret to like him! And everybody tried to make a good impression.

Brian's shoulder brushed another as they left the dance floor, and Dane turned to inspect the person who had bumped into him. Those cool grey eyes travelled over Brian from perfectly styled hair to gleaming black patent shoes, and then rested on the perfectly tailored velvet dinner jacket as he asked, 'Red, do you know this person?'

'Of course I do,' she snapped.

'That's a comfort. I didn't want to have to throw out a gatecrasher.'

'Who would want to gatecrash this sort of affair?' Brian snorted.

Dane's grey eyes made another leisurely assessment. 'You did,' he said gently.

Jenny clutched Brian's arm. 'Brian, this is Dane Sutherland. He's the manager of the bakery, and my stepbrother.'

Dane smiled. 'So I'm back in the family again. I do wish you'd make up your mind, Red. It's so exhausting never to know where I stand; I feel like a ping-pong ball sometimes.'

'My heart just cries for you. Dane, this is Brian Randall.'

'Of course—the almost-fiancé. I do hope you're properly grateful to me. If I hadn't told you what was going on, you'd still have been back East thinking that all was well with your little romance.'

'Thank you!' snapped Brian. 'I believe I can handle my affairs all by myself.'

'Affairs?' Dane's tone was properly shocked. 'Why, Red, you never told me!'

Brian started to bristle, and Jenny slipped a hand up around his neck to tug his head down. 'Ignore him, Brian, please just ignore him,' she whispered into his ear. 'He's only a troublemaker.'

'Love secrets, Red?' Dane drawled.

'He insulted you, Jennifer!'

'And no doubt I will again some day,' Dane

agreed. 'Hasn't my—little sister—told you that we don't get along, Brian? I must excuse myself and look after my guests now. But remind me during your stay to tell you why we seem to fight all the time. I think you'll enjoy the story, Jennifer was quite amusing when she was seventeen.'

And he moved away through the crowd.

CHAPTER SEVEN

JENNY SAT ON the carpet in front of the fireplace, hugging her knees, watching the flames dance and listening to the soft rise and fall of Margaret's voice as she read from *A Christmas Carol*. At Jenny's side lay the black kitten, his stomach rounded from a recent meal, slapping the air with his paws as he chased an invisible prey. She suspected that Lucifer would rather have had a bright-coloured Christmas ornament from the tree that twinkled in the bay window, but Margaret had put her foot down.

Across the room, Richard sat, his eyes closed, in pyjamas and robe. Usually it was he who read this classic each Christmas Eve, after the stockings had been hung up, but though he was much improved after just a few days at home, he still tired easily. Jenny was certain he wasn't dozing off, though, for now and then he looked over at Margaret with a loving sparkle in his eyes.

Jenny tickled Lucifer's ribs and hoped fervently that when she was Margaret's age someone would be sitting across the room on Christmas Eve and looking at her with that same sparkle. Would that someone be Brian? She looked up from the fire and caught his eye. He looked bored as he tapped his fingers on the arm of his comfortable chair, but that was only to be expected. Brian was accustomed to being busy every minute, with decisions to make and carry out, and after four days of enforced idleness, it was only natural that he was bored.

Jenny was surprised that he had agreed to stay for Christmas; but then, she decided, her father had almost forced the issue. And she was glad that Brian had agreed. She wanted him to get to know her father, and she wanted Richard's approval of her choice. If, she told herself firmly, Brian was her choice, for he had still not proposed. He had said nothing definite about marriage since his comment that Rosemary planned to announce their engagement at her first big party of the spring.

Finnegan got up from his place beside Dane's chair, shook himself, and came over to Jenny as if to investigate why she found the flames so intriguing. Lucifer hissed, and the big dog backed away, trembling. After his nose had been well scratched, Finnegan had learned that the little kitten was an opponent to be respected. Lucifer watched the dog back off and arrogantly started to wash himself.

Jenny looked up again and found Dane's eyes on her, a question that she couldn't read in the brooding grey depths. That question, whatever it was, was Dane's problem, she told herself with a tiny shrug. He'd spent most of the last few days at his cabin; tonight was the first he had been at the house for dinner since Richard had come home. It had made it easier for them all, but Jenny wondered why he had chosen to isolate himself so. Unless Suzanne was also spending her time at the cabin, she thought cynically, and concluded that that was very likely.

The only one missing from the family circle tonight was Aunt Agnes. She had firmly declared that Dickens bored her to extinction and had retired to the kitchen to make peanut brittle. Nobody dared object—Aunt Agnes was something of an outlaw—but Brian had looked as if he'd rather go along than join the family by the fire.

Finnegan loosed a fierce volley of barks, startling Jenny so that she jumped. The dog tore across the room to the front windows to defend his people from the intruders he was sure lurked outside. Dane pulled aside the drape and glanced out of the window. 'You nitwit,' he told the big dog. 'It's only the Christmas carollers from the church.'

Jenny scrambled to her feet and went to open the front door. The group of young people, perhaps twenty in all, arranged themselves around the front steps and began to sing. 'Oh Come, All Ye Faithful,' the young voices rang out, blending in the sheer joy of being alive. Jenny stepped out on the porch, and the old melody reverberated around her as they sang the carol and then repeated it in Latin. She wasn't aware that Dane was beside her until the song ended, and he reached up to wipe a tear off her lashes.

'Don't get all soggy,' he recommended. 'You'll freeze that way.'

Margaret came to the door. 'Come in, everybody,' she invited. 'I just happen to have punch and cookies here...'

There was laughter from the group. 'Homemade or from the bakery?' one of the men called out.

'Is there a difference?' Margaret asked innocently. 'Come in and warm up, now.'

Alison flung an arm around Jenny's shoulders. 'You'll freeze without a jacket out here,' she said. 'Why don't you come carol singing after all? We're going to the nursing home next, and then to the hospital. After that we go back to the church for hot chocolate before Midnight Mass. Come on, we can use another strong soprano.'

Alison had invited her earlier, but carol singing just didn't seem to be Brian's sort of pastime. As bored as he looked right now, though, he'd probably jump at anything, Jenny thought.

Margaret had heard Alison's invitation. 'Go if you like, Jenny. Richard's tired anyway, and I think he needs an early night. If you go carol singing, he won't be so tempted to stay up.'

'If you insist...Brian?'

He groaned. 'Whatever you say, Jennifer. I can't believe what I'm doing. I just hope the newspapers don't get hold of it!'

Brian didn't see the sudden gleam of humour in Dane's eyes, but Jenny did, and she glared at him.

'Remember all the years we spent in choirs, and madrigals, and glee clubs?' Alison asked.

'You were always flirting with all the boys instead of singing,' Jenny accused.

'I know. That's why you always got solos and I didn't.'

Dane tapped Jenny on the shoulder and held up her ski jacket.

'Are you anxious to get rid of me?' she asked as she slid it on.

'Not at all,' he said calmly. 'I was ordered to go along too. Mother is cleaning house—getting rid of all her problem children.'

Jenny looked around and quipped, 'In that case, where's Aunt Agnes?'

'Maintaining a low profile with the peanut brittle. And no one can move your Aunt Agnes if she doesn't want to move, anyway. You know that, Red. It runs in your family.'

But going carol singing seemed to be no great hardship for Dane after all, and though he made a few wisecracks he didn't seem to mind. When Jenny looked around it took only an instant to see the reason. Suzanne was hanging on to his arm as if it were a life-raft.

'Suzanne, I can't put on my coat when you're holding my arm,' Dane protested mildly, and she released him just long enough to let him put his parka on.

With a last flurry of thank-yous to Margaret for the cookies and punch, the group straggled out of the

Ashley house and began 'We Wish You a Merry Christmas' to a couple of strollers who were walking across the street.

'You're not singing,' Jenny said to Brian as he walked along beside her, shoulders hunched against the cold and hands deep in the pockets of his cashmere topcoat.

'Never could enjoy that kind of thing,' he muttered.

'What? Singing, or Christmas carols in particular?'

'Oh, all this holiday hocus-pocus. I'd just as soon forget the whole thing. Rosemary had the right idea— go to the Caribbean and let somebody else fuss about putting up the tree.'

'Wait till Jenny goes to work on you,' Alison warned. 'Maybe someone should tell you: this is the original Christmas kid. Name a tradition, and Jenny will engrave it in gold for all to follow. And then she makes up a few of her own from time to time.'

'I'm not that bad, Alison,' Jenny protested. 'I hate to Christmas shop.'

'How many people did you buy gifts for?' Alison demanded.

'Only about thirty.'

'I'd hate to see what she'd do if she liked to shop,' Alison pointed out.

Jenny just shook her head.

'What do people do in this town for entertainment?' asked Brian, a note of disgust in his voice. 'Is Christmas carolling all there is?'

'Of course not,' Alison said brightly. 'We could

always run down to the cow-calf conference at the armory.'

'Or the market barrow show,' Jenny added. 'Or the conservation tillage display. In season, of course.'

Brian put his hands over his ears.

'What's so bad about agriculture?' Alison questioned. 'Just where do you think your basic sirloin steak comes from, anyway?'

'It just sounds so frightfully rural,' he explained.

Alison looked as if she was about to enlarge on the topic. Jenny nudged her and picked up, in her clear soprano, on 'Oh, Little Town of Bethlehem.'

Alison took the hint and joined in, her rich alto blending perfectly. The snow had started again, and great clumps of flakes drifted down and caught in Jenny's hair, which was streaming down her back. She'd been in too big a hurry again to find her hat.

She saw the snowflakes dust on to Dane's dark hair, where he walked just ahead of her, bent over the fair head so close to his. The pair seemed to be doing more whispering than singing. Jenny told herself tartly that Dane was certainly old enough to choose his own entertainment. But she wondered if he really realised what he was letting himself in for.

The Midnight Mass was as majestic as she remembered it from her childhood, the bells and the rich rolling chords of the organ sending chills down her spine. She was still shivering from the after-effects of the old ritual when she and Brian got back to the

house. The living room was warm and dim, the firelight flickering down to embers.

Brian shot a look around the room, then took
Jenny's coat out of her hands, flung it over a chair,
and swept her into his arms. 'I thought I was never
going to see you alone again,' he complained. 'How
do people get to know each other around here, anyway? We're always tripping over someone.'

'Like this,' said Jenny. She locked her hands together at the back of his neck and pulled his head
down.

'What a wonderful idea,' Brian murmured as his
lips met hers.

It was a long, tender kiss, and after he raised his
head he continued to hold her close, his hands warm
on the curve of her hips. He nibbled her earlobe and
murmured, 'You smell so sweet tonight. New perfume?'

'No. Margaret's again. She always has all the latest
stuff.' Jenny's voice was husky.

'She has good taste.'

'Better than you do, at any rate,' Dane said cheerfully. He was standing in the doorway to the kitchen,
holding a dish heaped with chocolate ice cream. 'You
really shouldn't kiss Jenny in public, Brian. You just
never know what will happen, or who might be
watching. And Mother has strict house rules, anyway.' He stirred the ice cream idly.

Jenny tried to pull away, but Brian's hold tightened. 'I see no reason to be embarrassed,' he told her

stubbornly, and turned to Dane. 'Jennifer wouldn't do anything her stepmother wouldn't approve of.'

Dane's eyebrows raised. 'Perhaps you don't know Red as well as you think you do,' he suggested sweetly.

Brian lost his temper, and Jenny slid out of his arms. Brian hardly noticed, but her action won a sardonic grin from Dane.

'That's the last time I'll stand by and listen to you insult Jennifer!' Brian sputtered. 'I don't know what your problem is, Sutherland—'

'It may just be indigestion,' Dane said thoughtfully. 'I dislike having to swallow your kind of pomposity.'

Brian plunged on. 'But as Jennifer's future husband, I demand satisfaction!'

'Pistols at twenty paces?' But Dane's eyes were on Jenny as she climbed the stairs. 'Why didn't you tell me it's now official, Red? He finally came up to scratch, hmm? Where's the rock?'

Jenny turned halfway up the stairs and leaned over the banister, her voice low and furious. 'You know quite well it isn't official, Dane, so stop aggravating me! And if you two want to go ahead and kill each other, help yourselves. I don't think you need a witness!' She flounced up the steps, making her exit in a way that Alison at her most dramatic would have envied.

'MERRY CHRISTMAS!' The greeting boomed out as Dr Grantham came through the front door, bringing a burst of frosty air and the scent of pine needles with him. Open house at the Ashleys' on Christmas Day meant precisely that; no one answered the doorbell because guests were expected to come right in.

Jenny was in the living room, which was standing room only with old friends and employees, drinking eggnog and sampling all of the hors d'oeuvres that Muriel had spent the last week making.

She looked up with a smile and went to greet the newcomers in the doorway, her long skirt swishing as she walked, the honey-coloured velvet blazer that she had found under the tree that morning bringing out the gold highlights of her hair, swept up into a knot on top of her head today.

'Hi, Doctor. Hello, Mrs Grantham. May I take your coats?'

The doctor was already out of his, and as Jenny reached for it he caught her hand. 'Well, well, well,' he said. He held up her hand for his wife's inspection. 'Look what we have here, Edna,' he said. 'You were right the other day, it seems. Pretty ring, my dear.'

Jenny smiled self-consciously as she looked at the elaborate cluster of diamonds on her left hand. 'Thank you, Doctor. It is beautiful, isn't it?' Even if she would have liked to help pick it out, she told herself, and even if she would have preferred a simpler setting, it was a gorgeous ring, and it must have cost Brian a fortune. He'd hinted that when he'd slid it on her finger this morning, beside the Christmas tree.

'I'm going to claim a kiss from the bride, my dear,'

Dr Grantham said, and gave her a hearty smack on the cheek. 'We wondered after we saw you at church the other day if there wouldn't be an announcement soon.'

Jenny shook her head in confusion. Was she so transparent that people could see an engagement coming just by looking at her?

'And what happier day to announce it than Christmas?' said Mrs Grantham. Her soft voice was even quieter in contrast with her husband's carrying tones. 'Richard and Margaret must be delighted.'

'They're very pleased.'

'Of course they are!' Dr Grantham beamed. 'Best sense you've shown in years, Jenny. I'm delighted you'll be staying with us after all. Dane's a lucky man.'

His words dropped into a sudden silence in the living room, and every person in the house heard the doctor's booming accolade. The grandfather clock in the hall struck ten, and the moments seemed to stretch for ever.

'I certainly am the lucky man,' Dane drawled from the fireplace, where he was leaning against the mantel, little Molly in his arms. 'You see, I'm not the prospective groom, Doctor.'

Jenny glared at him. 'There's no need to be rude, Dane,' she snapped.

He shrugged. 'Not rude, darling. Just incorrigibly truthful.'

She saw Brian across the room and beckoned him

for an introduction, still furious at Dane. Now she understood, of course, what Mrs Grantham had meant. She must have seen them in church the day Dane had made such a production of sitting there with his arm round her. The poor woman was red-faced, but nothing ever bothered the doctor.

'I'll take back everything I said about good sense, Jenny,' he commented as he watched Brian come across the room, elegant in a perfectly tailored three-piece pinstriped suit. 'Are you certain your father is pleased?'

'Yes, of course he is. Brian won't be able to stay, of course, but we won't be married until autumn anyway, so there'll be plenty of time for preparations after I get back.' Jenny's chin was raised defiantly as she introduced Brian, who was at his most charming.

The charm rolled off Dr Grantham, though, who merely grunted a few times and then said, 'Young man, you're more fortunate than you'll ever realise that Jenny Ashley was born shortsighted. I wouldn't recommend you wait till autumn to marry her, or she might regain her senses.'

Jenny started to bristle, then, with an effort, she forced her anger back into a dark corner of her mind and smiled.

'It isn't very flattering, is it?' Dane agreed at Jenny's elbow. He handed Mrs Grantham a glass of eggnog. 'If I were Red, I'd be a bit offended that my young man was willing to wait almost a year. I'm afraid I'd start thinking I wasn't as important to him as the business cycle or the social season.' The baby in his arms cooed and reached for Jenny. When she was ignored, Molly settled back against Dane's shoulder and put her thumb in her mouth.

'But you're not me,' Jenny reminded him pointedly. 'And you can mind your own business. I don't envy the woman who tries to put a wedding ring on your finger!'

'Don't you?' Dane asked quietly.

'And I positively pity the woman who succeeds!' Jenny snapped, and walked away.

Alison was at the punchbowl. She looked sharply at Jenny and said, 'Here, let me fill that glass; you're so mad you're shaking, and you'll spill it all over.' She poured the eggnog and asked, 'Want some rum in it?'

'No, thanks. All I would need is a couple of drinks and I'd really tell Dane what I think of him!' Jenny sipped and caught the thoughtful look in Alison's eyes. Jenny laughed. 'Besides, I wouldn't want Finnegan to feel left out if I was drinking and he wasn't allowed.'

'Is that dog still hitting the bottle?'

'Only when no one is looking.'

Alison thoughtfully stacked used glasses on a tray. 'Are you so angry because Dane is right?'

Jenny choked. 'Right about what?'

'About Brian not being very anxious to be married, if he's willing to wait almost a year. After all, Jenny, there's no real reason to wait. You're both adults.'

'Brian has excellent reasons for waiting till next fall.'

'Then there must be something else you're upset with him about,' Alison said thoughtfully.

'Brian? The only person I'm mad at is Dane, and if he doesn't shut up about this whole thing I'm going to punch him!'

'No,' Alison disagreed. 'You ought to be speechless with happiness. And you're not. You're angry.'

Jenny didn't bother to answer. She picked up the tray of used glasses and started for the kitchen. At least there everyone would leave her alone.

Margaret was basting the turkey, which was already golden-brown and was beginning to give off the luscious aroma that Jenny could still remember from holidays long gone. Christmas was Margaret's day to shine; she could cook a turkey that was the envy of the state.

She looked up with a smile. 'Is the house still full?' she asked.

'Oh, yes,' said Jenny. 'Why don't you go back in with your guests? I'll keep an eye on things out here.'

'Thanks, Jenny. There really isn't anything that needs doing right now, though. That's the beauty of turkey dinners; all the hard work can be done the day before.' Margaret shut the oven door and stood up, brushing a hand across her flushed cheek. The emerald on her right hand caught her eye as it gleamed in the light. 'Thank you for my ring, dear.'

Jenny shrugged. 'Daddy bought it.'

Margaret grinned. 'It's fairly obvious who chose it, though. I appreciate it.' She gave Jenny an impulsive hug. 'You don't seem very happy today, though, I thought with that new ring on your finger you'd be dancing on the furniture.'

But of course Margaret hadn't witnessed the scene in the living room a few minutes ago when Dane had been so rude, Jenny told herself. Well, she wasn't going to be the one to fill her stepmother in. 'It's just all the people, I think.'

'It would have been nice if you'd had a little private time with Brian first, wouldn't it?' Margaret agreed. Not even the tone of Margaret's voice implied a hint of criticism.

Jenny wondered if she herself was overreacting to wish that Brian had not put that ring under the Christmas tree. She'd always imagined that when the time came she would get her ring in private, just the two of them together in some special spot that meant a great deal to them both. But to open it in the middle of a family Christmas, with her father and stepmother looking on…with Dane looking on… It had taken her by surprise.

'Well, there'll be all afternoon,' Margaret consoled. 'Your father and Dane will be so absorbed in the football games they wouldn't notice an air-raid. So you and Brian can do whatever you wish.' She took a pitcher of eggnog from the refrigerator. 'By the way, Jenny…' Her voice was suddenly hesitant. Jenny looked up questioningly. 'If you'd like to call your mother, go ahead. Richard doesn't mind, honestly he doesn't. And though we're enjoying having you here, we don't want her to feel left out.'

'I guarantee you that Rosemary's not feeling left out,' said Jenny. 'She's the life of the party on that cruise ship. And she's uncomfortable when she has a daughter around. It makes her feel old.' She looked around the warm, aromatic kitchen. 'This is the first Christmas I've had in five years.'

Suddenly she was in Margaret's arms. 'I'm so glad you're here with us, Jenny. You belong here.'

They held each other for a long time, letting their closeness soak away some of the hurts of the past. Finally Margaret let Jenny go and reached for her handkerchief. 'Goodness, aren't we a pair?' she asked.

'I'm glad we are,' Jenny agreed. 'You'd better get back to your guests before they think you've fallen into the oven!'

'Coming?'

'In a little while. I'll just clean up some of the mess.'

Margaret didn't insist. Jenny loaded the used glasses in the dishwasher and washed some of the party trays, all the while thinking about the way she wanted to celebrate next Christmas, the first in her new home with Brian.

Dane came in a few minutes later, when she was refilling the snack trays. He brought in a stack of empty eggnog glasses and arranged them in the dishwasher. 'Everybody is wondering why you ran away, Red,' Dane said eventually.

Jenny turned her back, trying not to see his tall body, in dark brown corduroy trousers and another ski sweater from what seemed to be an endless supply, this one a matching brown with a cream design. 'I wasn't running away. I wasn't needed in there, and I am doing something useful out here.' She reached into the refrigerator for a bowl of dip.

'I owe you an apology, Jenny,' he said as he closed the dishwasher and turned it on. He leaned against it, arms folded across his broad chest.

Jenny's eyebrows raised in shock. 'Do you mean you even know what the word means? The wonderful Dane Sutherland?'

He smiled. 'That makes us a pair, doesn't it? We're both dogs—you're an Irish setter and I'm a...'

'Great Dane,' Jenny finished. 'Why ever didn't I think of that before?' She put a handful of crackers on the tray and looked up. 'What's the apology for? I can't wait much longer. I've held my breath as long as I can.'

'I'm sorry I assumed that the emerald ring you were sporting the other day was yours.'

'You assume a lot of things that aren't true, don't you, Dane.' She studied the tray she was arranging and added some radishes for effect.

'You make it easy to jump to conclusions, Red. But I shouldn't have assumed that you'd put the bite on your dad for emeralds.'

'Actually, I did put the bite on him, as you so elegantly phrase it. He'd never have bought an emerald, even for Margaret, if I hadn't pushed it. She seemed to like it, didn't she?'

'That's a safe assumption,' he said dryly. 'Any time a woman cries when she opens a Christmas gift and then shows it off to everybody who steps into the house, I think you can conclude that she likes it.'

Jenny started on another tray. 'She deserves pretty things. And she likes them so much that I like to see her get them.'

Dane had moved so quietly that it startled her when he spoke, so close to her that his breath tickled her ear. 'I'm glad you're wearing my perfume, Jenny.'

'Yours? It's not aftershave, Dane. Margaret gave me this—you saw me unwrap it this morning. I borrowed so much of it from her I guess she thought I needed a bottle of my own.'

His laugh was soft. 'Where do you think she got it, Jenny?'

'Did you give it to her? Big deal!'

'Not only gave it to her, darling. Made it for her, with my own little hands.'

Jenny didn't comment. She just reached for the nearest dishtowel, wet it under the tap, and started to scrub the perfume off her throat.

Dane laughed at her. 'You'll never get it all off like that,' he said. 'It's formulated to stay on. Not a very practical product for sales purposes, actually—it lasts too well.'

'It's worth a try,' Jenny snapped.

'And I'd also judge you've put it on a few places that you won't wash off with me standing here watching. He took her hand, pushed the sleeve of the velvet jacket up, and held her wrist to his nose. 'You didn't get rid of it all,' he said, and kissed the pulse point.

She tried to pull away, but his grip tightened. 'Why do we waste so much energy fighting each other, Jenny?' he asked softly. He continued to hold her wrist, his other hand teasing at the lapel of her jacket.

A curious laziness spread over her as she stood there. She hadn't been so close to him since the night of the Christmas party when they had danced together. She stared up at him, knowing there was nothing in the world she could do to keep him from kissing her, knowing that if she struggled in his arms he would enjoy subduing her, and knowing too that some primitive part of her would enjoy being subdued. What was wrong with her? she wondered frantically.

But he didn't kiss her. He merely stood there, so close to her that she could feel every breath he drew, and outlined her face with the tip of his finger, each touch a slow caress, as if he were memorising every feature and preparing to sculpt her.

'If Brian sees us like this, he'll kill you,' she said in a perfectly normal conversational tone.

'Are you sure he won't kill you instead,' he asked, his hand slowing for an instant. 'After all, you're the one who's engaged to him, and you aren't exactly struggling.'

'What good would it do me to struggle?' Jenny asked.

He grinned. 'None. But we can't expect Brian to know that.' His fingertips completed their tour, and he cupped Jenny's face between his palms and turned it up to his.

'Don't underestimate Brian,' she warned, hardly knowing why she said it.

'Maybe you should warn Brian not to underestimate me.'

'Why don't you like him?'

'Do you mean it shows?' Dane mocked.

'Don't tease. I want to know. What is there about him you don't like?'

'I'll tell you something I like about you—Mother's perfume. But it needs a little something extra to be just right for you.' He pondered an instant, nuzzling her throat to get the full effect of the fragrance. 'I know. A little more musk—this isn't quite sexy enough for you to wear. And Brian's cheap. That's one of the things I don't like about him.'

Jenny waved her left hand at him. 'This didn't exactly come out of a cereal box, Dane.'

'But it did arrive on Christmas. Any man who puts off a proposal till Christmas so he doesn't have to buy another gift is just plain cheap.' He snatched a kiss so quickly that she didn't have time to dodge, and was gone.

CHAPTER EIGHT

'DO YOU HAVE your long underwear packed?' Jenny asked as as Alison, her winter coat and gloves already on, cuddled her baby.

Alison handed Molly back. 'Why do you persist in thinking we're going to freeze up at the cabin? It's heated—and it's not exactly primitive.'

'Besides,' Jim added, 'who said I was going to let her get out of bed all weekend?' He leered at Alison, who put her hands on her hips and told him to shut up.

Jenny waved goodbye to them from the picture window, waving Molly's little hand as well, and then carried the baby back to the kitchen where Brian was drinking coffee. She stopped in the doorway to savour the feeling of domesticity, the weight of the baby in her arms, the smell of the fresh-perked coffee, the sight of Brian relaxing with his cup and the morning paper. It brought a tug to her heart as she thought how lucky Alison was.

She put the baby briskly down in her high chair and strapped her in. 'Let's have breakfast, shall we, Molly?' she asked, and reached for the cereal Alison had left on the range. Molly babbled and giggled between bites, and her joy in finding a new day to savour was contagious.

Jenny didn't realise how much noise the two of them were making until Brian slammed the coffee cup down on the table and snapped, 'How is a man supposed to read a newspaper around here—much less get anything important done?' He hit the newspaper against the edge of the table and walked out of the kitchen.

Jenny absently spooned cereal into Molly's mouth and said, 'I wonder what's wrong with him?'

Molly babbled a string of sibilant syllables and then nodded her head like a little owl.

Jenny laughed. 'No doubt you're right—whatever it was you said,' she told the baby as she started to clean her up. By the time she had bathed Molly and wrestled her into a stretch terry playsuit, Jenny was wondering how Alison ever managed to get anything done.

Brian was staring out of the front window on to the quiet street, where flakes of snow were once again drifting down through the frigid air.

Jenny put the baby down to play on a blanket and went to stand beside him. 'Brian, I'm sorry we were making so much noise,' she said, wondering if that was what was really bothering him.

He turned to smile sadly down at her. 'It's all right, Jennifer, I'm just not used to being around kids.'

'Maybe this is a good time to start,' she said

lightly. 'In a couple of years we may have one of our own.'

'Good heavens, Jennifer, let's wait till we're married before we start planning on having children!'

'You do want children, don't you, Brian?'

'I suppose I'd like to have a son. But there's no hurry about it, as far as I'm concerned.'

Jenny opened her mouth to argue, and Brian laid a finger across her lips. 'Jennifer,' he said firmly, 'it will be a whole year before we're even married. Why get wrapped up in an argument about how many children we're going to have?'

Jenny gave in. 'It does sound kind of silly, doesn't it? It's just that I don't want to wait till I'm so old I have to have nannies to take care of my kids. I want to do it myself.'

'You'll be busy with the other things that will be required of you, Jennifer.'

'What kind of things? Charities and fund-raisers and all that sort of rot like Rosemary occupies her time with?'

'You'll be far too busy to have time for a job, Jennifer.' Brian sneezed.

Her belligerent stand faded before her concern for him. 'Have you caught a cold?' she asked.

'I must have. Damn this Iowa weather!' he cursed, and sneezed again.

'Here, come and sit down and I'll fix you a cup of tea.'

'I don't want a cup of tea. A shot of whisky would be a lot better for me.'

'Are you sure?' Jenny asked warily. 'I'll see if Jim has any.' As she turned to leave the room, she saw Molly struggling to get her feet under her. As Jenny watched, fascinated, the baby raised up on her toes and her hands and slowly straightened up, wobbling and weaving as she tried out this new balancing trick.

'Oh, look!' Jenny cried. 'Alison said yesterday that Molly hadn't stood up by herself yet. And there she goes!'

Brian didn't even glance up. 'Whoopee,' he said. 'Were you going to look for a drink for me, or shall I have to get up?'

Molly lost her balance and plopped down on to her blanket, the diaper cushioning her fall. She looked mildly surprised, then rolled over on to her back and started to pull at her shoestrings.

It wasn't that Brian wasn't interested in the baby, Jenny told herself as she searched through Alison's cabinets. And if Molly had been his own child he'd have been applauding every step of the way. Wouldn't he?

The afternoon dragged. While Molly napped, Brian dozed in his chair, and Jenny did the dishes, wondering what had happened to her cheerful domesticity of the morning. 'Maybe you're not cut out to be a housewife,' she mused. 'Same routine, over and over…'

But that was the very reason why she didn't want to get involved in the social affairs her mother pre-

sided over, either. There was very little difference between a tea to benefit crippled children and one to
promote the next governor of the state, and Jenny
found them all to be crashing bores. For her own sake,
she would prefer to be out there teaching the children
to walk. Brian would come around to the idea of her
working, she told herself fiercely. He simply had to.
If she tried to be a social butterfly, she would not
only be a flop, but she'd be climbing the walls from
boredom as well.

Brian woke up about mid-afternoon and after a few
ill-fated attempts at conversation, Jenny suggested he
go home and go straight to bed. He was too miserable
to argue.

By the time Jenny had tucked Molly up in the tiny
crib that night, she was exhausted herself. No wonder
Alison needed a break, she thought. Molly had been
into more mischief than Jenny would have thought
possible for an eight-month-old baby. The child
wasn't even walking yet. Jenny didn't envy Alison
the job of keeping Molly out of trouble.

She took a hot bath and put on one of her Christmas gifts, a dressing gown of heavy silk. She felt
wealthy just wearing the luxurious robe. She brushed
out her hair and left it loose. There was no one to
see, and she intended to be comfortable.

With a book and a cup of hot chocolate, she tucked
a blanket around her legs and curled up on the end
of the couch. She was only into chapter two when the
doorbell rang.

She put the door on the chain and let it open a few inches. 'Forget it,' she told Dane, who stood on the step with his hands in his pockets. 'Margaret always told me never to open the door to suspicious characters.'

'I have a message from your semi-beloved.' As she continued to hesitate, he said, 'Don't want it? All right, I'll go away.'

Jenny sighed and opened the door. Dane carefully locked it behind him, draped his coat over a chair and went into the living room to warm himself by the small wood stove.

'How long is this message, anyway?' Jenny asked dryly. 'You seem to be making yourself right at home.' She curled up on the couch and pulled the blanket up around her.

'You don't need to cover yourself up, Red. I've already seen the whole show.' He turned to baste himself in the heat of the fire. 'Brian said to tell you that he's never been so miserable in his life and that it's all your fault because he had to come out here to this godforsaken hole.'

Jenny reached for Alison's guitar, which leaned against the end of the couch. 'Did he really?'

'Approximately, though it took him a lot longer to say it.'

She strummed a chord and adjusted the tension on a string. 'He didn't look well when I sent him home.'

'It's only a cold, Red. From the sound of him, you'd have thought it was typhoid. A hypochondriac and a cheapskate,' he mused. 'What a combination you've found yourself!'

'You could have told me that on the phone. So what is it, Dane?'

He pulled a folded sheaf of paper out of his pocket. 'I found this on my desk at the bakery this morning. I assume you left it yesterday.'

Jenny strummed another chord and decided the tuning job would pass. 'Actually, I left it three days ago. But I should have known better than to think you might stop in on Christmas Day. Or the day before. Or even the day after.'

'I do not do my best creative thinking at a desk,' he told her.

'That reasoning must come in handy.'

Dane gave her a penetrating stare. 'Do you want to discuss this memo of suggested changes to the bakery, or don't you?'

Jenny yawned. 'I'll be at my desk at eight on Monday morning.'

'I won't be. Now or never, Red.' He dangled the memo between two fingers and looked from it, to her, to the small wood stove.

'Go ahead and burn it. I'll just make another copy.' But she capitulated. 'I suppose this is the only way to get rid of you.'

'You're a quick study. Let's start with the cookie names. Why do you want to change them?'

'It's in there. "Grandmother's Old-Fashioned Raisin" doesn't make it in the eighties.'

'Well, "Raisin Swirls" doesn't do anything more for me. Keep trying.'

'Yes, sir.' Then his words sank in. 'Do you mean it, Dane? I can really change the names?'

'Only if it's an improvement,' he warned.

'It will be. We can change the whole atmosphere of the company by renaming the products!' Jenny leaned forward in her excitement and caught Dane's glance at the low neckline of her gown. She clasped a hand to her throat, trying to make the gesture look casual.

He laughed, but looked down at the list in his hand. '"Gingerblocks" I can live with. But what's this "Chocolate Dumps" thing?'

'That's those chocolate drop cookies that are so popular.'

'I assumed that. But—'

'It's a better name than the one Steve and Jim were batting around the other day. They wanted to name them "Big Bird Cookies."'

Dane put a hand to his forehead. 'I don't think I want to hear this, but go ahead.'

'Because Jim said they looked like a big bird just flew over and…'

'Try again, Red, and leave Jim out of it this time.'

'I liked it myself.' She shrugged her shoulders at his look. 'I'll try again. What about the frozen dough production and the dry mixes?'

'I hereby appoint you a committee of one to investigate thoroughly and submit a report. And I mean thoroughly, Jenny. No half-page summaries of how great an idea it is. I want facts.'

'Yes, sir!' Jenny snapped her best salute.

'When you've submitted a report, we'll consider where we go from there. Now that that little matter is taken care of…' He folded the memo and returned it to his pocket, then came to sit beside her on the couch, his legs stretched out and his hands in his trouser pockets.

'I don't think you were invited to stay,' Jenny said primly.

He grinned. 'Sure I was. Alison asked me to keep an eye on you and the baby. How is Molly, by the way?'

'Well, I haven't beaten her up yet.' Then she remembered the day's good news. Maybe Dane would appreciate it. 'She stood up all by herself today.'

'She's early to do everything. Neat kid. I wouldn't mind having her around all the time. Can I peek in at her?'

'She's asleep.'

'I didn't say pick up, I said peek at. But I won't argue, I'll just choose another activity.' Dane settled back into the corner of the couch and began a leisurely survey of Jenny, his eyes roaming over her body with the intimacy of a touch.

Hot colour climbed in her cheeks and she fussed with the blanket, re-draping it. 'All right, go and look at the baby,' she ordered finally.

'I've changed my mind. I'd rather stay here and

look at you,' he said softly. Then his mood changed abruptly. 'You should have been home for dinner. The parents dropped a bombshell.'

'Oh?'

'They didn't mean to, of course. They were going to wait till you were there. But the secret slipped out.' He stretched his feet out again. 'Mother's found an apartment in that new complex downtown, and they're moving as soon as Richard's health will stand it.'

'But why?'

'Because the complex has a gym and an indoor swimming pool and an elevator, and the apartment is small and easy to keep up, and they're tired of living in a big house that they can't take care of. That's it in a sentence; it took all of dinner to discuss it properly.'

'It makes sense,' Jenny admitted. 'What are they going to do with the house?'

'It's been sold.'

Jenny sat up straight. 'Without a word to the rest of the family?'

'Without a word to you, don't you mean? I can't imagine you being upset that they hadn't told me. What do you care? You won't be living in Twin Rivers.'

'They could have told me.'

'They didn't think it was any of your business, and they're right—it isn't. Now, it is my business, and I have a right to be upset.'

'Why?' Jenny asked starkly. She looked at the bottom of her hot chocolate cup and got up to put the kettle on so she could make more.

Dane followed her to the kitchen. 'Because I'll have to seek out a new home.'

'I always did think it was odd that you continued to live with them. It was cheaper that way, right?'

'Not exactly.'

'Now you can just move out into the woods with the rest of the animals and you can all be happy together.'

'You've never seen my cabin, have you?' Dane asked lazily.

'I've never been invited.'

'And you probably won't be, either,' he agreed. 'That looks good,' he commented hopefully as she poured the boiling water over the hot chocolate mix.

Jenny sighed and got out a second cup. She dipped whipped cream on to the surface of both cups and sprinkled them with cinnamon. She pushed Dane's cup towards him, but he ignored it and watched as she took a sip from her own. Whipped cream smeared over her upper lip and she stuck out her tongue to lick it off.

Dane took the cup from her hands and set it on the counter. He cupped her chin in his hand and said, as if the idea had just occurred to him, 'You really don't do it on purpose, do you?'

'Do what?'

'You have no idea how seductive you are. That

little trick with the whipped cream… You really don't know how that affects me, do you?'

'No. If I had, I wouldn't have done it. There's nothing I want less than to seduce you.'

Dane didn't seem to hear. Jenny couldn't have moved away from him if her life had been threatened. He was holding her there with his gaze, hypnotising her with his eyes. He traced the outline of her lips with a gentle finger.

'Didn't you hear me, Dane?' she asked breathlessly. 'I don't want you to be interested in me. And as for you—you couldn't turn me on with a switch!'

He raised an eyebrow. 'That's a challenge you shouldn't have issued, Jenny.'

He took his time about kissing her, starting with featherlight kisses on her forehead, her earlobes, down her throat to the deep slit that passed for a neckline. Always his lips were gentle, teasing. Jenny struggled in his arms, and Dane caught her hands, held them behind her back, and continued to caress her with his mouth.

'Do you have a thing about kitchens?' she gasped.

'No,' he said softly, raising his head for an instant. 'I just have a thing about you, wherever you are. But if you'd rather go somewhere else…' He lifted her off her feet and carried her down the hall towards the master bedroom.

'Put me down!' she squealed.

'Very well.' Dane obliged and dropped her on the bed. He was beside her in an instant, loosening her robe so that her slim body was bare to his gaze. His hands skimmed over her creamy skin, bringing gasps of pleasure. Then he ran his fingers through the long strands of her hair as it straggled wildly over the pillow, and muttered, 'Your hair, Jenny, your gorgeous hair. You don't know what it does to me just to see your hair tumbled like this for me.' Only then did he kiss her lips.

She had been waiting for that kiss, Jenny realised as she lost herself in the sweetness of his mastery. She had been longing for it, and now that she was at home in his arms again, she sighed deeply with pure pleasure and pulled him even closer, giving him back kiss for kiss with a passion that she had only suspected lay hidden within her. Her body was screaming for fulfilment.

Dane pulled back, and since Jenny's arms were locked about him, she was dragged halfway across the bed as he stood up.

'As an experiment,' he said coolly, 'I think it could be called a success.'

Jenny's words were slurred with passion. 'What does that mean?'

'You said I couldn't turn you on with a switch. Well, you're not only turned on, darling, you're glowing like a neon sign. I think I've proved my point.' He found the sweater he had discarded and pulled it over his head. 'Don't you think you'd better cover yourself up?'

'Why? You've seen everything there is to see.' She

scarcely heard herself. Dane had kissed her like that, held her, come so very close to making love to her, just to prove that he could?

He reached across her and picked up her left hand. 'I'll leave you with something to think about, Red,' he said. 'If a woman is wearing a man's ring, and yet enjoys herself so very much with another man, maybe she'd better take the ring off.' He stalked out of the room.

Jenny struggled to her feet and followed him down the hall. He was zipping his parka as she caught up with him at the door.

She leaned against the wall and folded her arms. 'You could have made love to me then,' she said, her voice still not quite steady.

'I certainly could have.'

A moment's silence. 'Why didn't you?'

Dane laughed. 'The eternal question, with a slight difference in phrasing!' He tipped her face up and was suddenly serious as he answered. 'Because, dear Jenny, tomorrow morning you would have been screaming that you'd been coerced. When I make love to you—and believe me, I will—it will be your own choice, and you will have no excuses to use the next morning.' He reached for the sash on her dressing gown and pulled it tighter. 'Sleep well, Red,' he mocked.

A swirl of winter air hit her in the face as he closed the door behind him, but Jenny's heart was colder still.

MOLLY STARTED to scream halfway through the church service on Sunday morning, so Jenny was already standing at the door when Margaret and Dane came out. Dane saw her waiting and smiled, a self-satisfied little grin that Jenny would have liked to remove with sandpaper. But she ignored him and turned to Margaret.

'How's Brian?' she asked.

'He's feeling better this morning,' Margaret said, 'but he didn't want to come to church. He said he'd be over to see you later, unless you'd like to bring Molly for the afternoon.'

'No. She's so fussy I think I'll take her straight home.' Jenny bounced the baby in her arms. 'I think she needs a nap. Or she may be coming down with a cold. Alison will love me for that!'

'It looks as if she didn't sleep any better than you did,' Dane put in softly. He reached for the baby, who went eagerly into his arms, babbling nonsense syllables. He cuddled her and made silly noises back at her, and Molly giggled.

'I slept just fine,' Jenny retorted, her tone giving the lie to her words.

'You need a couple of days off, Jenny.' Margaret sounded worried. 'We'll have you down sick too if we aren't careful.'

'I'll take a nap when Molly does,' Jenny promised and put a quick kiss on Margaret's cheek. 'I'm off to the nursery again. Tell Brian I'll expect him this afternoon.'

'I thought you were going to take a nap,' said Dane. 'Or are you inviting Brian to join you? And by the way, Red...I like your hair when it's pinned up like that.' The words were innocent enough, but the expression in his eyes made the compliment almost seductive.

'Thanks,' Jenny said curtly. She reached for Molly, who didn't want to leave Dane.

'You might have to take me home, too, Red,' he said. His hands closed over Jenny's on the soft fur of the baby's snowsuit. It was an intimate gesture, the handing of the child from one to the other, and they stood there for several moments as if glued together by the contact.

Molly went down for her nap without protest, and Jenny curled up in a quilt in the living room to watch an old black and white movie on television. But most of her mind was occupied in thinking—as she had thought all through the night—about what had happened to her last night in Dane's arms.

Was there something wrong with her? Was she promiscuous, to have responded so passionately to a man she didn't even like—and her stepbrother at that? She was engaged to Brian, and she enjoyed it when he kissed her. But that was nothing like last night had been. Dane could have made love to her, and she wouldn't even have protested. It wasn't easy to admit that to herself, but it was true. All he had to do was touch her and her morals evaporated.

She turned off the TV and stalked down the hall to

the master bedroom, where she sat down at Alison's dressing table and stared at herself in the triple mirror.

It wasn't strictly true that she hated everything about Dane, she admitted to herself. There were things she liked about him. Most of them only occurred to her when he wasn't around, she told herself, and forced a laugh.

But there were more things that she didn't like about him. She hated the way he acted as if she belonged to him. She hated the way he treated her. 'And you hate the fact that he walked away from you last night and went home to go to sleep like a baby,' she told herself. He'd said once that he didn't think Jenny had ever been truly awakened. Well, he'd taken care of that last night. She was wide awake now, and tingling with every sensual inch of skin and nerves. And Dane had walked away, satisfied because he had won the challenge.

And he had probably gone to Suzanne's apartment and told her all about the joke he'd just played on Jenny, she fumed. He'd told Jenny that she was seductive and that he wanted to make love to her, and then he'd walked away.

What was it he had said about her hair? Something about liking to see it tumbled around her, just for him to see. Jenny looked at it in the mirror, pinned up in a smooth twist, and pulled out the hairpins ruthlessly, heedless of whether strands of hair were caught, until it cascaded down around her shoulders in a glorious fall of red-gold highlights. So he liked to see it this way, did he? she thought vengefully. That, at least, was something she could change.

The scissors lay next to her hand, and almost without volition she picked them up. Three swift blows, and the long red strands were piled in a heap on the glass top of the dressing table.

Then she looked at the heap of hair, at the scissors in her hand, and at the ragged remains at the nape of her neck, and started to sob like a child.

She cried as she dialled the telephone, and when Margaret answered, Jenny wailed, 'You have to come, Margaret. I need you right now!'

'What is it, darling? Is Molly all right?'

'Yes. Just come, Margaret, please hurry!'

Margaret drove the few blocks to the Riley house in record time, and Jenny met her at the door, her head wrapped in a towel.

'What's wrong, Jenny! Have you hurt yourself?' demanded her stepmother.

Jenny didn't say a word, just slowly pulled the towel off her head.

'Oh, my God…Jenny, have you gone completely crazy?' Margaret walked around her, surveying the damage. 'Whatever came over you, to cut that beautiful hair?'

Jenny started to sob again.

'Well, whatever it was, the damage is done. Let's see what we can do to salvage it.'

'Can you do anything, Margaret?'

'Honey, even a professional would regard you as a

challenge. And I'm pretty rusty. But come along and we'll see.'

Two hours later Jenny studied herself in the dressing table mirror again. Margaret put down the electric curling iron with a flourish. 'It will take some getting used to, Jenny, but I think it's pretty,' she said. 'At least you left a little length so we could get a curl into it. And it has enough natural curl to hold up well, once it's relieved of all that length.'

Jenny studied the close-cropped curls and said flatly, 'I look like Little Orphan Annie. And I feel worse.'

'If you're wise, you'll make an appointment for a permanent wave tomorrow. Then it will grow out gracefully, and in a year or so it will be long again. And who knows? You might like it short. It will be a lot easier to take care of than when it was way past your shoulders.' Margaret sat down on the edge of the bed. 'Now, let's have it. What on earth made you pick up those scissors? I thought kids outgrew that by the age of five.'

The silence lengthened. Finally Jenny said sullenly, 'I cut it because Dane said he liked it long.'

Margaret started to laugh. 'I'm sorry, Jenny,' she gulped, and rolled over on to the bed. 'I just can't help it! You two are such nitwits!'

'Thanks,' Jenny said awfully. The doorbell rang, and she hurried down the hall to answer it before it woke Molly. Margaret followed.

As Jenny reached for the doorknob, she added,

'And if you tell him I said that, I'll…' There was no threat dire enough.

'Won't breathe a word,' Margaret promised, sliding into her car coat. 'I just hope I'm there when he sees it.' She kissed Jenny's cheek. 'And believe it or not, I actually do like it.'

'That makes one of us,' Jenny muttered.

Margaret stopped in the kitchen. 'By the way, Muriel sent a message. You told her she'd like Brian?'

'Yes?'

'She doesn't,' Margaret said cheerfully, and went out through the kitchen.

Jenny opened the front door to find Brian on the step.

He stared at her for a few moments. Then he exploded. 'What in the bloody hell have you done to your hair, Jennifer?'

'Made it easier to take care of,' she explained, 'Margaret thinks it was a great idea.'

'Then Margaret has lost her senses!'

'Oh, come on, Brian, I'm still the same person whether my hair is long and straight or short and curly.' She led him into the living room.

'Rosemary will kill you!' he exploded.

'By the time I see her again, it will have grown six inches. And would you mind talking a little more quietly? I don't want to wake the baby.'

'That's what I came to talk to you about this afternoon, Jennifer.'

'The baby?'

'No, Rosemary, I called her this morning, and she's very upset at the idea of your staying here all winter.'

'I expected she would be, Rosemary is frequently upset by some of my ideas. Brian, there are some things we need to talk about.' Jenny braced herself. She should tell him about Dane, she knew. It wasn't fair to him not to let him know. And perhaps if she told Brian, the whole thing would look foolish again, and she could laugh about it.

'What is there to talk about?' His tone was deep with suspicion.

Jenny instantly lost her nerve. If she told him what had happened last night, he would never believe that it had stopped there. She couldn't truthfully say that Dane had forced anything on her, but if she told Brian that she had been a willing participant, he would never trust her out of his sight again. She swallowed hard.

'There are things that we've never discussed. We need to talk about it now, before we're married. The decision on having children, for one thing.'

He shrugged. 'You want a child; fine, we'll have a child. Just not right away.'

'But what does that mean, Brian?'

'It means that you're twenty-two years old. You can have a baby any time in the next ten years.'

'The later the better?'

'From my point of view, yes. You'll be a great asset to me, Jennifer. I need you as a hostess, I need your contacts through clubs and social functions. You can't be doing that if you're at home nursing a baby.'

Jenny was silent for a long time. 'What about my job?'

'You quit it to come out here. It obviously was not very important to you.'

'So you don't want me to work, either.'

Brian shrugged. 'I think it's silly, but if you insist on working, you can do public relations for my company in your spare time. It'll keep you occupied, and the company could use the help.'

'That's not the same.'

'I don't see what's so bad about it, or even with volunteer work. We certainly won't need for you to be bringing in a pay-cheque. I earn a good salary, and Rosemary will increase your allowance when we're married. She knows you'll have extra expenses.'

'Having a husband is an expensive luxury, is that it, Brian?'

'We'll be living on a little higher scale than you've been doing, Jennifer. You won't be sharing an apartment with three other girls any more.'

'And that comes expensive, doesn't it?' Jenny didn't wait for an answer. 'What about my father, Brian? Will I be able to visit him, or will I just say goodbye when I leave here next spring?'

'Rosemary won't object to you visiting, I'm sure.'

Jenny pounced. 'So it's what Rosemary wants that's most important to you, isn't it, Brian?'

'She wants what's best for you. She wants you to

come home immediately so that our engagement can be announced in January.'

'Rosemary wants, Rosemary thinks! What about what I want?' Jenny snapped.

'You owe it to her, Jennifer. She's your mother, after all.'

Jenny studied his expression. 'Is there anything else Rosemary wants?' she asked, keeping her tone carefully casual.

Brian grabbed at the neutral tone. 'I'm glad you're going to be open-minded, Jennifer. She thinks it would be a good idea to move the wedding up—June, probably. And why you had to cut your hair when you could have had it so beautiful for the wedding...'

'Let's leave my hair out of it, Brian, and concentrate on Rosemary.' Jenny sat down, her legs crossed just so, as Rosemary had taught her, her chin in her hand in the thoughtful, listening pose that Rosemary had told her made such an impression on a man. 'And if Rosemary didn't want us to be married in June?'

'Then we'd wait. She is your mother, after all, Jennifer. We owe her our co-operation.'

'Jenny stared at him thoughtfully. Things were starting to add up. 'Just how much do you owe her, Brian?'

He looked puzzled.

'What is she going to do if I don't come back?'

He was hesitant, but he finally said, 'She was making noises about writing you out of her will.'

'Hmm. And if Rosemary disinherits me, where

does that leave us, Brian? Do you want to marry Jenny Ashley, or Rosemary's heiress?'

'This is insane, Jennifer. Why won't you just show some common sense and come back with me? You're coming in the spring anyway. Why not come now and keep Rosemary happy?'

'Because I've spent five years trying to keep Rosemary happy, and I haven't had any great success.' Jenny walked across the room and stared out into the bleak December afternoon. 'Did Rosemary tell you she would increase my allowance after the wedding?'

'She implied it,' Brian said stiffly.

'I suggest you come straight out and ask her. Because you see, I haven't taken an allowance from her since I graduated—the very minute I was able to be self-supporting.'

'She will, Jennifer. She wants you to come home. She said she'll give you the prettiest wedding any girl ever dreamed of—she even has your dress picked out, and it will cost a fortune.'

'Don't you see, Brian? That's just it. I don't want Rosemary to choose my wedding dress. I don't want her to choose anything for me—especially my husband!' She pulled the diamond cluster of her finger. 'I suppose Rosemary chose this, too.'

'She certainly didn't,' he said stiffly.

'But you showed it to her before you bought it,' Jenny challenged.

'Of course I did. What's wrong with that?'

'Nothing, if you didn't care what she thought of it.

But you did care, didn't you, Brian? You'd have fallen in love with me if I'd been bald and hunch-backed, so long as I'm Rosemary's heir. What if I'm not, Brian? What if I'm just Jenny Ashley, with a job in Twin Rivers, Iowa, as the public relations director of a bakery?'

The answer lay in his eyes. He turned away guilt-ily, then wheeled back to face her. 'Jennifer, it would be so easy... She just wants you to come home, dar-ling.'

'That may be all she wants right now, Brian. Do you know how many times in the last five years I've heard that threat? Join the best sorority, Jenny, or you'll be disinherited. Get elected president of the debutantes, Jenny, or you'll be cut out of my will. It was never so obvious, of course, but it was there. How long do you think it would be before it happens again?' She held out a pleading hand, trying to make him understand. 'I've lived the way Rosemary wanted for five years. Now I have a choice, Brian, and I'm going to live my own life.' She turned the ring in her hand, then held it out. 'I think it would be better for both of us if you didn't try to persuade me.'

He took the ring reluctantly. 'I suppose you're right, Jennifer. I really wish it could have been you.'

Her heightened intuition made the leap in reasoning instantly. Brian had her replacement already in mind. 'Good luck to you, and to whoever is number two on your list,' she said tartly.

In the nursery, Molly started to scream, and Jenny

turned to go to her. She didn't watch as Brian left the house.

If a woman is wearing a man's ring, and yet enjoys herself so much with another man, maybe she should take off the ring.

Dane's words echoed in her mind as she changed Molly's diaper. 'Oh, stop it, Jenny,' she told herself crossly. What Dane had done and said last night had nothing to do with her action today.

The tears that she shed were hot, angry ones, tears that cleansed the wound and left it free to heal.

CHAPTER NINE

SUZANNE LOOKED UP from her typewriter as Jenny came in, still wearing her coat and stocking cap. Then the secretary pointedly stared at the big wall clock. Its hands read fifteen minutes past two, and Suzanne smiled malevolently as she told Jenny, 'The boss wants to see you right away.'

'What's his hurry?'

'I don't know. He told me to give you the message the instant you showed up.'

'Sounds like Dane. Where is he hiding this afternoon, in his lab?'

'No. He's in his office.' Suzanne gestured over her shoulder.

'You're kidding. I didn't think he knew where it was.'

Suzanne shrugged and picked up her coffee cup. 'You'd be surprised. I'll be in the coffee room.'

Only because the office was soundproof, Jenny thought. If Suzanne thought she could hear the lecture she was so certain Jenny was about to receive, she wouldn't budge from her desk.

Jenny tapped on the solid oak door and was still waiting for an answer when Steve came in.

'Are you just coming to work?' He crossed the office to stand beside her.

'Why is everyone so upset? I asked for the morning off because I spent all weekend babysitting. Has it been declared a crime not to come to work on Monday morning?'

'Dane's been a little upset all morning,' he explained.

'Too bad it's so rough on him. If I'd known it would affect him like that, I'd have asked for the whole day.' She pulled off her knitted mittens.

'I see you aren't wearing your ring any more,' Steve observed.

'No. We decided to call it off. Must have been the shortest engagement in history.'

'I'm glad you broke it off. I never could bring myself to give you my congratulations.'

'I noticed,' Jenny said gently.

'He just wasn't right for you. Will you be staying?'

'I suppose so. There's nothing for me to go back for now.'

'Can I take you to Alison's New Year's Eve party?'

Jenny smiled. He really was a dear boy. 'Sure, Steve. I'd like that.'

Steve pushed the door open and let her precede him. Dane was sitting at his desk, feet propped on the edge of it, a coffee cup in his hands, staring out the window across the frozen Iowa landscape. He looked up. 'Make yourselves at home. You could have taken time to hang your coat up, Red.'

'I was told it was urgent.'

'Well, it wasn't that urgent. It's waited all morning.'

'You gave me the morning off yourself, Dane, and you know it. If I've missed anything important, you have only yourself to blame.'

'I only gave you the morning off because Mother insisted you were going to be sick if you didn't get some rest.'

'It's sweet of her to worry about me, isn't it?' Jenny's tone was flippant, but she had been grateful to Margaret that morning when, with one look, her stepmother had sent her back to bed and called Dane. It wasn't that Jenny had felt so awful, but the weekend had exhausted her, so she had let Margaret have her way.

'Isn't it? But you don't look sick to me.'

'So take it up with Margaret. Or are you accusing me of grafting on my sick leave?'

'You can't be. Short-term employees don't get any. Perhaps it's just that you're already missing Brian?'

'Did Margaret tell you he'd gone home?' she asked.

'I have all kinds of sources.'

'It must be snowing again,' Steve put in, trying to sidetrack the argument. He brushed a finger over the snowflakes still clumped on Jenny's green stocking cap. Not a strand of red hair showed under the hat. 'I think I'm going back to Arizona.' He hunched his shoulders against an imaginary cold draught.

'It snows there once in a while too, and they aren't prepared for it,' Dane said absently. 'Iowa hasn't even got a good start yet. Shall I make it an order, Red? Take your coat off and make yourself comfortable.'

If Margaret had told him she thought Jenny wasn't feeling well, had she also confided in him about the new hairstyle? Jenny dropped her mittens on the floor beside her chair. What would Dane's reaction be when he saw her close-cropped curls? Would he be angry when he saw the lengths to which she would go in an effort to displease him? Or would he just think it was funny to have succeeded once more in forcing her to react to his teasing?

She took a deep breath and pulled off the dark green stocking cap.

Steve gasped disbelievingly as her hair, instead of tumbling wildly halfway down her back, sprang forth in disordered ringlets.

Dane merely regarded her with a raised eyebrow and said, 'What I wanted to talk to you about, Red, is that Steve has volunteered to help you with that report we talked about over the weekend.'

'The one about the frozen doughs and dry mixes?' Jenny struggled out of her coat and draped it over the arm of a chair.

'Did we discuss any other...reports?' he asked sweetly.

Jenny flushed. 'No, that was the only one.'

'Steve can be especially helpful when you start doing a financial analysis. I suggest you take him up on his offer.' He drained his cup. 'I'll expect to have the report by Friday afternoon, Red.'

'By Friday? When there's another holiday in the middle of the week? You're crazy, Dane!'

'Management doesn't get holidays, Red. You've told me several times that you plan to take my job from me. Perhaps if you found out what's really involved you wouldn't want it so badly.'

'I don't see you missing out on holidays,' she retorted. 'And as for being on call all of the time... You were up at the cabin again last night, weren't you?'

'How would you know?'

'You certainly weren't at home.'

Dane smiled. 'And you really think there's nowhere else I could go?'

Jenny flushed. 'I suppose that means you were at Suzanne's apartment. Well...'

'Not necessarily. And you can leave Suzanne out of it.'

'Protective, aren't we?' Jenny jeered.

'As a matter of fact, I was right here last night. All night.'

'And whose choice was that?' His eyes were red, and he looked tired, she thought.

Dane stood up. 'Report on my desk by Friday afternoon, Red.'

'I just can't have it done by then!'

'If it isn't, I shall have to conclude that you aren't as interested as you originally seemed.'

'But...'

'You've already had two days, Jenny,' he said sweetly.

Jenny opened her mouth to protest, then reconsidered. It would do her no good to argue, as usual, Dane held all the cards.

He opened the door and stopped at the threshold. 'I'll be in the lab for a while if anyone needs me, Steve. And by the way, Red, I like your hair that way. I've always wanted to see what it looked like cut short and curled.'

He vanished down the hallway. Jenny looked wildly around for something to smash. If it couldn't be Dane's skull, she thought viciously, she'd settle for something softer—like the varnished-brick wall.

Suzanne had witnessed the whole scene. She was sitting at her desk, one hand held daintily over her mouth as if trying to disguise a smile.

Jenny picked up her coat, cap and mittens, stormed into her own office, threw them down on a chair, and wheeled on Steve, who had followed her. 'Well, what do you want?' she asked angrily.

'I thought if you wanted to start on that report... I guess it will wait,' he said awkwardly, and backed out of the door.

Jenny tossed herself down in her desk chair and indulged in a few minutes of pleasant dreaming about what she would have done to Dane Sutherland if she had been a member of the Spanish Inquisition and he had been a heretic. But the daydream, pleasant as it was, couldn't last. She sighed and reached for a clean notepad and a pen.

She might not have noticed the noise except that she had looked up from the first draft of her report to think about where she might find some of the information she would need. Dane would probably have it at his fingertips, she fumed, and if she didn't get it right, he'd know it instantly. Suzanne might be able to put her hands on it, but Jenny doubted that the secretary would try too hard. She flung her pen down and rubbed her temples wearily.

Then the bang sounded, and the building seemed to give a little shudder. It wasn't a loud noise, actually; if she had been concentrating she might not have heard it. She wondered idly what it was, but the pressure on her to have this report done made her pick up her pen again.

The door opened so fast it slammed against the wall, and Suzanne burst in. 'There's been an accident,' she cried. 'Steve needs you at the back of the building immediately!'

Jenny was on her feet instantly. If it's Steve who's calling for me, she thought in that first frozen instant, then the bang I heard must have been something exploding in Dane's lab.

Steve was disappearing down the hall as she reached her office door. Suzanne was standing by her desk, knuckles pressed against her mouth.

'Don't just stand there, do something,' Jenny ordered. 'Call the cops. Call an ambulance, for heaven's sake!' She followed Steve down the hall.

But he passed the closed door of the lab at a run and went down the stairs two at a time into the shipping room. Jenny's heart rate slowed a little and she followed, seizing a first-aid kit off the wall as she passed.

From the doorway, she could see what had happened. A semi-trailer truck which had finished loading and was attempting to pull away from the loading dock had caught a wheel on the ramp and toppled on to its side. It lay almost against the building, blocking the entire approach to the loading area, the trailer crumpled. Dozens of loaves of bread and packages of cookies lay scattered around the dock.

Steve and another man had climbed on top of the cab and opened the door to try to reach the driver. The man had been bounced around, but as Jenny watched, he pulled himself from behind the wheel and they hoisted him out of the cab. He was bleeding from a scrape on the side of his face.

'My boss is gonna kill me,' he was muttering as they got him to the ground.

Jenny handed Steve the first-aid kit and turned back towards the building, suddenly aware of the biting sleet that had started to fall. She shooed the employees back into the building. 'The excitement is all over. The police and ambulance will be here soon. Everybody go back inside and stay out of the way.'

They did so reluctantly, and Jenny was shivering

by the time she herself got back to the warmth of the building. And if she was cold, she thought, what about Steve and those who were helping him out there in the rain and sleet without anything warmer than sports jackets? And meanwhile, where was the boss? Concentrating on an experiment that would be ruined if he left it? Perhaps he hadn't even heard the excitement.

She stopped beside the door of the lab, staring resentfully at it. Everybody thought Dane was so marvellous, she thought scornfully. Well, where was he when he was needed? Playing with his test-tubes!

She pushed open the door and went in.

It was a well-equipped little lab, scrupulously clean and without so much as a scrap of glass tubing out of place. So much for her early suspicions that Dane's alleged lab was only a hideaway with a comfortable chair and a good book!

Jenny had taken only the required chemistry courses in school, but she knew enough about the subject to realise that this was a lab many full-time scientists would envy. 'Of course it is,' she mused. Dane would never have anything second-rate; it was probably because of the near-poverty he had lived in as a child. Now he bought the best he could afford. 'And with access to Ashley money, he can afford the best,' she told herself. It was apparent, however, that Dane was nowhere in the room, so she closed the door carefully behind her and went back to the office wing.

Steve was sitting on the corner of her desk. 'Thanks for taking care of the crowd,' he said. 'The poor guy was in bad enough shape without having an audience.'

'How is he?' she asked.

'They took him to the hospital, but it was only a precaution. He broke his nose, and scraped up his face. Nothing major.' He sipped his coffee. 'He's probably right, though—his boss will no doubt fire him. A guy who can't get a truck away from a loading zone without hanging up a wheel shouldn't be driving a rig that size.'

'What about the building? Was there any damage?'

Steve shook his head. 'Maybe to the dock—we won't know for certain till they get the truck moved away. But if it had to happen, it picked the best time. That was the last truck of the day, so there's plenty of time to clear it out before we have to load tomorrow's shipment. If there'd been six lined up back there as usual, we'd have had dominoes.'

'That's some comfort. Meanwhile, where was the boss when all this was happening?'

'Dane? He went up to the cabin to be sure Jim and Alison left it in good shape. And before you get all upset at Dane, remember, I'm the assistant manager. When he's not here, this is part of my job.'

'He went to the cabin?'

'Jenny, he didn't know the kid was going to tip a truck over at the loading dock. Be reasonable!'

'I'm just sick of Dane being here three hours a

week and everybody defending him, saying how well he runs everything. As far as I can see, he isn't running anything!'

'Jenny...'

She had her coat on by the time he'd slid off the desk. A moment later she was standing beside Suhanne's typewriter.

'I'm leaving the office now, and I won't be back this evening,' she announced.

'Going home to pout?' Suzanne had regained her calm exterior. It was the first time Jenny had seen her all day that she had had time to notice Suzanne's expensive suede blazer and silk blouse. She certainly did dress well, Jenny reflected. The secretary fitted the cover over the typewriter with exaggerated care and reached into the bottom desk drawer for her handbag.

Jenny stopped dead. 'What would I be pouting about?'

'How many things can there be? It must have really hurt when your dad sold your little dream cottage on the hill to Dane, didn't it? I hear you didn't even get a chance to say anything about it.'

Dane had bought the house? But he had seemed so irritated about having to move. Jenny remembered how careful he had been about saying the house had been sold. He hadn't said anything about how it had been done so quickly and quietly.

Suzanne went on, 'It's probably a good thing for you that you won't be here next summer. I imagine it would really make you mad to see me moving in there. Just think, Jenny—in high school I wasn't good enough to wipe your feet on, and now I'll be living in the house you always thought you'd inherit. It just goes to show what happens when people think they can come back after five years and take up just where they left off.'

Jenny stared at Suzanne, seeing the venom in the girl's eyes. No, she wouldn't lie about that. It would be far too easy to check. All Jenny had to do was go home and ask Margaret. Suzanne was telling the truth! Dane had acquired the Ashley house, as he had acquired control of the bakery, the foundation of the Ashley fortune. And he had pulled off the coup under her very nose.

The sleet was falling even harder as Jenny darted across the parking lot to her car. It felt like tiny knives slicing into her cheeks. Fortunately, her car had been cold when the storm started, so the windshield was only partly covered, not iced over completely. Jenny scraped it, letting the defroster run to heat up the interior. When she slid behind the wheel the car was warm.

The street had been sanded, and she could feel the snow tyres on her little car take hold in the roughened surface. Traffic was heavy as workers headed for home early or made a trip to the supermarket before the storm pinned them in. But Jenny wasted no time in wondering why so many cars were on the street.

She threaded her way through the traffic, her lights

reflecting back from the needles of sleet, and turned west on the main highway leading out of town. Oak Grove Park was fifteen miles west of the city, and in that area was Dane's cabin. When she found it, Jenny planned to indulge in a large-scale temper tantrum while there was no Richard or Margaret around to stop her. It was time someone told Dane Sutherland what was what!

She rehearsed her speech as she drove, practising just what she was going to tell that insufferable stuffed shirt when she found him. Then her rehearsal was abruptly halted when the snow tyres grabbed for traction on a patch of ice on a narrow bridge, and the car spun out of control and careened sideways down the highway.

Long-unused training automatically took over. 'Steer into the skid, Jenny,' her father had preached. For hours at a time on the empty runways of an iced-in airport he had made her brake sharply, pull out of a skid, accelerate, pull out of another. Now the hours of torturous practice saved her. On the other side of the bridge, the ice hadn't yet frozen into a solid coating, and the tyres broke through to find some traction.

Jenny reduced her speed, said a fervent thank-you to her guardian angel that no one had needed the on-coming lane right then, and kept going. The wind had picked up and the sleet was coming down faster. Mixed in with it now were snowflakes, and her headlights reflected off the combination with a glare worse than fog produced.

And to think she could have been lounging on the deck of a cruise ship ploughing through the smooth waters of the Caribbean! Jenny told herself. Sitting beside the swimming pool in her favourite bikini, sipping a tall glass of pineapple juice. Or poking through duty-free shops in St Thomas for souvenirs. Or eating lobster thermidor at the captain's table. Or dancing with Brian after a nightclub show...

Brian. He'd been gone less than a day. Rosemary would really be angry when she returned from her cruise to find that Jenny had thrown over what was probably the best offer of marriage—by Rosemary's definition—that she would ever receive. Brian was a blossoming young executive; he already held a lot of power, and he'd be a wealthy man some day. Rosemary wouldn't understand how Jenny could toss that aside.

Jenny could remember how shocked she had been when she had first realised that Rosemary didn't love her husband. She'd been seventeen and she'd been living with her mother for just a few months. Until then, she had always excused Rosemary for deserting her, believing that she had left Richard for a man she loved. But Rosemary had merely looked at her as if reluctant to believe that this simple-minded child was really hers and said, 'Jennifer, love is cute. I don't know anybody who's against it. But love isn't the lubricant that makes the world go around—money is. Love wears out. Money doesn't.' And she had been off, a mink jacket tossed over her shoulders, to a Senator's house for cocktails.

No, Rosemary wouldn't understand why Jenny had given back that diamond ring. Rosemary had turned her back on a man who adored her and an infant who depended on her, because a wealthier man had come along. It was ironic that Richard's biggest success had come in the years right after Rosemary had left him.

Jenny looked at the mileage indicator. She had come almost ten miles, and the park should soon appear off to the right at the intersection of a gravel road. Surely the gravel was in better condition than the pavement; its rough surface would be harder for the ice to cover. And it was less distance to the cabin now than it was to return to Twin Rivers. She took a deep breath and kept going.

Half an hour later, she wasn't sure where she was. The snow was falling harder, so hard that sometimes she could scarcely see ten feet in front of the car. The mileage indicator said she had come another five miles, and she should be reaching the intersection soon. If, that was, she hadn't already passed it. It was possible, with the blowing snow, that she had driven by without recognising the park.

Her breath was coming faster, and her hands were clutched so tightly on the wheel that her knuckles ached. She tapped the brake lightly to slow even more so she could get a good look at the next intersection. But it wasn't the right one either, and she drove slowly on.

But had it looked familiar? Jenny's memory wasn't clear enough to be depended on. She'd been just a child the last time they'd picnicked at Oak Park; it had been a favourite gathering place for families and groups. But it was different to approach it in the sleet than to ride there carefree in the back seat beside the picnic basket.

There were no other cars on the highway. She'd met just half a dozen in the whole distance, along a stretch of highway that was normally one of the heaviest-travelled sections in the state.

'Maybe that ought to tell you something, Jenny,' she scolded herself. What a city slicker, to let herself be fooled by the weather conditions in town into thinking that the highways would be safe. Of course the highway was in worse condition than the streets in town; out in the open ice could build up faster and there were fewer cars to keep it beaten off the pavement.

The state road crews had thousands of miles to sand and salt. Sometimes visibility got so low during storms that the governor ordered the snowploughs off the roads till the snow and wind stopped. And here she was, fighting the storm alone in a compact car.

Another intersection, and finally she spotted the gnarled old trees that marked the corner of Oak Park. She breathed a sigh of relief, slowed the car, and turned down the small steep hill on to the gravel road. Then she let out a strangled scream as the car turned a complete circle on the ice. The first instinct of panic

was to lock her brakes, and the car rocked unsteadily
to the verge of the road before Jenny got control of
herself, took her foot off the brake pedal, and shifted
into low gear. The car stayed on the road but it slid
inexorably towards the bottom of the hill.

'All right, I get the message,' Jenny muttered, and
took a good look around. If she could get back on the
highway, she'd fight her way back to town. Obviously
she'd been wrong again; the gravel roads were not
only icier but they were narrower than the highway.

But the approach was too steep, and she didn't have
enough engine power to back the car up the slope.
Neither could she risk turning around on the narrow
road. The fact that the car had done a complete circle
and stayed on the road was more luck than any skill
of the driver.

So she took yet another deep breath, and suddenly
remembered that no one knew where she was going.
Even though Steve might have a good idea, no one
knew for sure, and she wondered how long it would
be before anyone asked where she was. She was in
this all by herself.

The gravel road was built over rolling hills, and
Jenny looked ahead to the first one with a shudder.
From a standing stop at the bottom, could she get
enough speed to top the crest?

She made the first two hills, but the third was too
much for the little car, and as she tried to back down
the hill to make another run for it, the tyres slid
slowly over the side of the road and down into the

ditch. Jenny carefully pushed the accelerator, but the car was firmly and finally stuck. It would not move until spring if it had to rely on its own power.

She sat there for a couple of minutes, stunned. Then she pulled herself together and took stock.

She was physically all right. Shaken, of course, but the car had ditched itself so slowly and smoothly that she hadn't even bumped her head. The car seemed to be all right, too, apart from the fact that it was no longer a means of transportation.

She looked at the gas gauge and groaned. Only a quarter of a tank; why hadn't she stopped to fill it today as she had planned? She tried to remember the standard survival lecture she'd heard so many times. Leave a window open a crack to avoid carbon monoxide poisoning; run the engine only for short periods of time; never start out with less than a full tank of gas.

'And make sure you never drive a car that doesn't carry a blanket and emergency food,' Jenny told herself wryly. Well, her slacks were wool—that was the closest she came to having a blanket. And there was a candy bar in her handbag that she'd bought on her way to work. What she wouldn't give to have one of Muriel's picnic baskets in the back seat today!

She looked at her watch, then looked again, shocked. It seemed impossible that it had taken nearly two hours to drive the fifteen miles she had come, yet her watch said it was after six o'clock. Margaret must already be worried about why she hadn't come home;

normally she was home by five. Jenny felt a sudden twist of guilt. Her father would be worried, too, and Margaret would be trying to hide her own concern to keep him from fretting.

And there was just no way to let them know she was all right.

Unless she left the car and walked, she would have to spend the night in a bucket seat. 'Nope,' she told herself. That had been the other main emphasis of the survival lecture: always stay with the car. Even if you were close enough to see shelter, a sudden worsening of the storm could cut visibility and leave you lost. The tales of prairie settlers freezing to death within yards of their own homes were true, Jenny knew. And it could still happen.

'How crazy can you be, Jenny Ashley?' she scolded herself. 'Driving out here in the middle of an ice storm that's rapidly turning into a blizzard to give Dane a piece of your mind, when you could have done the same thing tomorrow morning at the bakery!' She tilted the driving mirror so she could see herself. 'You'd better be careful about giving away pieces of your mind,' she mused. 'There's hardly enough left to keep you operating now.'

She broke off a piece of the candy bar and let it melt in her mouth. She'd never tasted anything so good. But then she hadn't had lunch, she remembered. There hadn't been time. She'd eat another piece of chocolate at eight o'clock, one at ten, and one at midnight, she planned. She'd have to stay awake, of course. Now how was she going to accomplish that?

It was dark, and she didn't dare run the car's lights; the battery wouldn't hold out long. 'That's all right,' she told herself. 'I don't have a book to read anyway.' She pulled her feet up under her on the car seat. It was warmer that way; the bottom of the car must be hugging a snow bank. She ran the heater for a few minutes, then resolutely turned off the motor. The sudden silence made her feel more alone than she had ever been before. She folded her arms across the steering wheel and stared out at the snow, now falling heavily and blowing in bursts across the road.

So Dane had bought the Ashley house, the house Jenny had grown up in, the only home she had known till she had gone to live with Rosemary. And he planned to live there with Suzanne. She tried the sound of it in the empty car. 'Next year at this time Suzanne Sumpter will be living in my father's house. If she wants to paint my room purple, that will be her right. If she wants to tear up the hardwood floors and strip off the oak woodwork and throw out all the antiques…' Had Dane bought Margaret's furniture, too? Or would Suzanne have the fun of doing it from scratch? Jenny shuddered and hoped she would never be invited to see the results.

Suzanne had been wrong about one thing, though. Jenny had never assumed that she would inherit the house. She just couldn't imagine a Twin Rivers without the big grey house on the hill, with her father and

Margaret at the door to greet her, with bread fresh from the oven, with the scent of Christmas in the air. She had never pictured herself living there again, but she had pictured bringing her children home for holidays with Richard. And now the residents would be Dane and Suzanne.

And Jenny, if she was going to stay in Twin Rivers, would have to find a place to live. That was what wasn't fair about it.

Lights swept across the car as another vehicle came down the hill. Jenny swung the door open and plunged out into the snow, waving frantically. Surely the driver would take her in. Maybe she could go back to town, or at least spend the night where it was warm and where she could call Margaret, so she wouldn't worry. Anything was better than freezing to death in her car.

The door of the jeep was pushed open from the inside, and Jenny climbed in. She was breathing hard just from the exertion of walking across the glare ice in slick-soled boots, and she sank on to the seat with a sigh of relief. 'Where are you going?' she asked. 'Not that it matters. I'm in no position to complain.'

There was an instant of silence. 'Hasn't anyone ever told you that hitch-hiking can be dangerous?'

Jenny's head swivelled so she could stare at the driver, a shadowy shape in the darkened vehicle. It was Dane.

CHAPTER TEN

JENNY SETTLED HERSELF with a little flounce and said, 'Believe me, it would have to be a pretty bad experience to be worse than spending the night stranded in a blizzard in a car that has three gallons of gas in it.' She caught the look he shot at her and added quickly, 'And don't give me the lecture about survival techniques. I know all that. It's just that I remembered it after I was stuck.'

Dane grunted his answer and put the jeep into gear with a short, savage motion. Finnegan reared up out of the back seat and washed Jenny's face with his tongue.

'I expected you'd be all tucked up in the cabin by now, watching it snow,' she went on. 'I suppose I should thank my lucky stars that you happened along.'

'You certainly should.' But Dane didn't sound interested. The jeep laboured up the hill, grabbing for traction on the ice.

'The four-wheel-drive really makes a difference, doesn't it?' Jenny asked brightly.

Dane didn't bother to answer. They topped the hill, and just over the brink he turned into a lane and pulled up beside an A-frame house painted a rusty brown. The little house looked as if it had grown there on the hillside, nestled into the pine trees.

'Are you choosing the very first place you can get rid of me?' Jenny asked. 'I don't mind. I can call Margaret.'

'No phone.' He got out of the jeep and slammed the door.

'But she'll be worried!' Jenny scrambled down and followed him to the house.

'You should have thought of that before you got this hairbrained notion to come out here.' Dane unlocked the door and stepped inside. 'Are you coming in?'

Jenny followed him unwillingly. 'Is there somewhere I can call from?'

'Yes. There are three neighbours within five miles. If they're home, that is, and if you care to walk. I've already driven nearly twenty miles on glare ice, and I don't plan to go out again until it melts.'

Jenny thought about it as she watched him kindle a fire in the big forced-air fireplace in the centre of the room. 'You certainly are making yourself at home,' she said finally.

Dane put a log on the fire and turned, a reluctant grin reaching his eyes. 'I am at home, Red. Just because a building is called a cabin it doesn't mean it's made of logs and has an outhouse, you know.'

'Oh!' She sat down on the arm of a chair and studied her surroundings with new eyes. So this was Dane's cabin.

The living area was one large room with furniture grouped casually around the fireplace. The chairs and couch looked as if they had been chosen for comfort rather than style, but the room was inviting. Shelves of books were everywhere. A big rug in an Indian design lay on the hardwood floor, and Finnegan flopped down on to it with an exhausted sigh, as if the ride over the icy roads had worn him out.

It was a man's room, with no ruffles or flounces. The wide windows in the front of the house were uncurtained; the view across the valley would be spectacular, Jenny supposed, if it wasn't blocked by the blowing snow.

Behind the living room a small kitchen was partitioned off by a half wall, and a short hallway led to the back door. On the opposite side of the hall was the only straight wall in the entire house, and on it hung another Indian rug, this one enormous and woven of brilliant colours. Above the back half of the house was a loft, reached by a spiral iron staircase.

Dane finished stoking the fire and turned, watching her survey of the cabin. 'Well?' he asked.

'Frankly, I expected a bunch of skins drying in the corner and a deer head mounted above the fireplace. But it's rather nice.'

'I don't hunt for sport, Red, so I don't display the trophies.'

'How anybody can kill a living thing…' Jenny shook her head.

'It's reasonably easy, especially after you've seen a grove of young trees deer have destroyed by sharpening their horns on the bark. Or a cornfield they've taken the best of the crop from before the farmer gets to it. Trees and corn are living things too.'

'But how you can look into those beautiful eyes and then…' Jenny shuddered artistically.

'Hunting keeps the population down so they don't starve to death. Would you rather see that happen? And speaking of starvation—are you hungry?' Dane asked prosaically.

'Famished! I forgot lunch.'

'There's the kitchen.' He pointed.

'Chauvinist!' But Jenny was too hungry to argue.

The tiny kitchen was a dream; every convenience a woman could imagine was at her fingertips. Of course, Jenny thought. Any son of Margaret's would have been taught to cook, and any man like Dane would see no reason to be without a labour-saving device if he could afford it. And Dane could obviously afford just about anything he wanted. She found an omelette pan in a well-stocked cabinet and put it on the stove to heat. No wonder he was careful who he invited to this retreat. It showed too much of what he really was.

'Do you want an omelette?' she called as she took eggs, cheese and a green pepper out of the refrigerator.

Dane answered from just behind her. 'Of course. Why do you think I picked you up out there instead of leaving you to freeze?'

Jenny made a face at him and started to break eggs. 'Why were you out there on the road?' she asked. 'If you don't have a phone, how did you know I was anywhere near? You certainly weren't surprised to find me.'

'I wasn't here. I tried the roads and decided against coming, so I went back to town.'

Jenny stopped in mid-motion with the eggbeater dripping. 'I drove all the way out here and you were at home?'

'You're making a mess,' Dane pointed out. 'I believe I've mentioned to you before this disagreeable habit you have of acting before you've put your brain in gear.'

'So why are you here now?'

'Mother panicked when you didn't turn up, and Steve said you'd flown out of the bakery making noises about me being at the cabin when I should have been working. It was fairly easy to figure out where you'd gone.'

'And you came out in this awful weather to find me?' The warm feeling that swept over her was absurd, Jenny told herself.

'Only because Mother was hysterical. Here, let me do that.' He lifted her bodily away from the stove, poured the eggs into the pan and expertly swirled it.

'You make the toast. You can manage that, can't you?' he mocked, and ruffled her hair.

He's treating me like his little sister, Jenny realised abruptly. And I don't like that either. But she resolutely pushed the thought away and found a loaf of bread.

The omelette was delicious, but midway through the meal the lights abruptly died. Jenny was startled and a bit frightened, but Dane matter-of-factly found a candle in a kitchen cabinet and lit it. 'I wondered how long it would be,' he said. 'The weight of that ice on the wires must be tremendous.'

'Does this sort of thing happen often?' she asked.

'About once a year. The power used to be off for days at a time out here, but not any more, they have good standby systems and it only takes a few hours.'

'A few hours?'

'That's what I said. Why? Don't you like candle-light? It makes you look even prettier, with the gold lights in your hair.' His voice was husky.

Candlelight is dangerous, Jenny thought, and got up from the table in a hurry. She picked up her plate and carried it over to the sink. 'Would you like coffee? I'll make a pot.'

'In an electric coffeemaker?' Dane mocked.

'Oh!'

'It's easy to forget, isn't it?' he asked. 'Electricity is such a way of life. We can boil water over the fire and make instant.'

'All right. I saw some teabags here somewhere, didn't I?' She started to run water into the dishpan.

'Just leave those. I'm thinking of putting in a dishwasher—what do you think?'

'I don't think you'd use it often enough to make it practical.'

Dane filled a kettle with water and took her elbow. 'Come on. Leave the dishes alone—you can't see them well enough to get them clean anyway. Come and sit down.'

Jenny knew she shouldn't. But she sank on to the couch before the fire, soaking in its delicious warmth, and watched him arrange the kettle over the flames. Finnegan dropped to the floor at her feet and rested his chin on her ankles. Dane put another log on the fire and came to sit beside her.

'I've been thinking this cabin lacked something,' he mused, and put an arm around her shoulders. 'I see you're not wearing that ring any more.'

Jenny's back stiffened. If he says anything sarcastic, she thought, I'll cry. And I don't want Dane to see me cry.

He massaged the tense muscles at the nape of her neck. His voice was very gentle as he said, 'I'm glad you showed Brian the door.'

'How do you know I'm the one who broke the engagement?'

'Because I know you very well, Jenny. You broke it off before he had a chance to.' He stared into the fire for a few minutes, and a brooding silence dropped over the room. Then he looked up at her and smiled, his eyes sparkling with laughter and firelight. 'It's nice here, isn't it? Just the two of us.'

'Don't forget Finnegan,' she reminded him.

'And Finnegan, of course. But just us, with no telephone to ring, and no one to interfere...'

She stared into his eyes, and somewhere in her mind the pieces of a jigsaw puzzle dropped silently into place. Of course, she thought with sudden blinding clarity. I don't want to be Dane's little sister. I've never wanted to be his sister. But it isn't because I hate him. It's because I want to be his wife.

Dane saw the change come into her face, and he was almost reverent in the gentleness of their first kiss. Jenny let her arms slide up around his neck and relaxed against him with a contented sigh.

She sat that way for a long time, drifting in and out of a dream, his kisses feathering down on her face, her throat, her hands. This, she thought, was what she was made for, to be in Dane's arms, to be kissing him and responding to the demands made by his body and her own, crying out for the fulfilment she knew they could reach together.

He had unbuttoned her blouse, and his hands were warm against her bare skin. He unfastened her bra and bent his head to caress her breasts, sending shivers of excitement down her spine. The desire in his eyes was plain. 'Please, darling, let me make love to you now,' he breathed against her lips. 'I want you, Jenny.'

Not love. Not even need. Just, 'I want you, Jenny.' And he would take her up to the loft where he had made love to Suzanne, and the other girls he must have brought here. What need did a man have of an isolated cabin unless he used it as a love-nest?

And what would happen after that? Jenny asked herself. What would she have left then? And why was he so insistent on making love to her when he was going to marry Suzanne? Was it because Jenny was the only part of the Ashley empire he hadn't yet conquered?

The kettle was whistling on the fire. She pushed Dane away and sat up, straightening her clothes. 'Do you make love to Suzanne like this?'

There was a momentary silence. 'Are you jealous?'

'No, I'm disgusted.' Jenny picked up the kettle and started for the kitchen.

'What's really wrong, Jenny?' he asked.

'The kettle will boil dry.'

'So let it boil. I'll buy a new kettle.'

She ignored him. 'I've been thinking about it,' she said calmly as she measured instant coffee into his cup and poured the boiling water over it. 'Perhaps you should buy a dishwasher. It will get you into the notion of being a home-owner. What are you planning to do with Daddy's house?'

He leaned against the side of the refrigerator and folded his arms. 'So that's what's bothering you!'

'You've really taken over the Ashleys now—right down to the ancestral home,' she said bitterly.

'I offered him exactly what the appraisal said it was worth, Jenny.'

'You must be proud of yourself!'

Dane shrugged. 'I don't see where pride comes into it. I like that house. Your father doesn't need it any more. And you, if you will recall, were planning at the time to move back East in the spring and never come to Twin Rivers again.'

'That's got nothing to do with it.'

'It has everything to do with it, Jenny. You don't want the house, but you don't want anyone else to have it either. You want it shut up as a museum for you to remember your happy childhood.'

'I just don't want you to have it.'

'Well, let me tell you something about happy childhoods, Jennifer Ashley. Yours wasn't happy. Your father adored your mother, and she treated him like a slave.'

'Leave Rosemary out of it!' Jenny said angrily.

'And my childhood wasn't happy either. But you were fortunate enough that your father was able to hire what was missing in your home. And I was fortunate enough that he came along and not only loved my mother but took an interest in me.'

'Quite an interest. That education of yours must have set him back thirty thousand dollars.' Jenny was horrified at the words she heard coming from her own mouth.

'Do you think I haven't tried to pay him back? He

won't take it. He laughs at me. I've paid him the only way he'll accept—by keeping the bakery running.'

'That seems to have benefited you as well.' Jenny looked round at the well-appointed kitchen. 'You've done what you set out to do, haven't you, Dane? The Ashley fortune is now a Sutherland fortune. The bakery is renamed so that soon no one will remember who owned it. The Ashley house will be known as the Sutherland house. The power is in your hands. And you did it right in front of me—that was the real fun, wasn't it? You took it away from me just to prove you could.' She let the silence draw out. 'I'm going to get some sleep. Do I take the loft or the couch?'

'Whichever Your Royal Highness wants,' Dane snapped.

'Then I'll take the loft. It's farther away from you.'

She stormed up the spiral stairs to the loft and flung herself across the bed—the bed, she reminded herself, that Suzanne slept in. Well, at least Jenny would sleep alone.

She cried herself to sleep.

SHE DREAMED THAT HE came to her in the night when she was cold, brushing the tears from her face and gently tucking her under the blankets, then holding her till the shivering stopped and she relaxed again.

Or had it been a dream? she wondered vaguely as she reached for consciousness.

Something tickled her nose, and she tried to push

it away. The tickle moved down across her throat and she reluctantly opened her eyes.

Dane was sitting on the edge of the bed with a duck feather, trailing it across her delicate skin. 'Wake up, sleepyhead,' he told her.

Jenny pulled the blankets over her head. The loft was bright with sunlight reflecting off the ice and snow outside, and it hurt her eyes.

'I'm going out to get wood. The electricity's back on, if you want to fix breakfast.'

She pushed the blankets down and abruptly remembered that she had taken off her slacks and sweater. She yanked the covers back up around her shoulders and noted with irritation that Dane, of course, had not missed a thing. 'Can we go back to town?' she asked.

'Not yet. There hasn't been any activity on the roads. By afternoon we should be able to make it.'

'Then why did you wake me up?'

Dane's tone was rueful. 'Because I thought you might wake up while I was gone and panic.'

'I think I could have survived the shock,' she assured him.

He lounged across the bed. 'Why were you crying last night, Jenny?'

'Crying?'

'Don't deny it. You're an awful liar, you know.'

'I was tired, and I was angry, and I was irritable,' she shrugged.

'Is that all?'

'That makes three good reasons, Dane. What do you want? A book?'

He lay back, hands clasped at the back of his neck, and said thoughtfully, 'You used to bring your problems to me to have them solved, Jenny.'

That was before you were my problem, Jenny thought. 'I was a child then.'

'Not exactly a child,' he disagreed. 'You were growing up, but there was a lot of child left.' He laughed softly. 'You used to cry till you got the hiccups, and then you'd put your head on my shoulder and just sit and let me talk to you till the sunshine came back.'

It was true; he could always make her stop crying. Unless it was he who had caused her tears. 'Speaking of sunshine,' she said firmly, 'the sun is out, and since I'm awake, I'd like to get dressed. Why don't you go get your wood and let me put some clothes on?'

'What if I prefer you without clothes?' But he got up, lazily, and stretched, catlike. 'The coffee's made, by the way.'

Jenny waited till his whistle had died in the distance before she got out of bed. She resisted the urge to look over her shoulder as she zipped up the wool slacks and pulled her sweater over her head. She'd be delighted to get some fresh clothes, she decided.

The view from the living room was as beautiful as she had expected; she poured her coffee and took it in to stand by the wide windows to look out across the valley. Sunlight reflected off the ice that coated the trees and wires. The pines that sheltered the cabin drooped under the weight of the ice, and on one of the heavy branches a male cardinal sat, his proud head jaunty as he surveyed his kingdom.

Dane came around the corner of the house with a bucket. He looked up at the window, and Jenny shrank back against the wall so he wouldn't see her there. He scattered the contents of the bucket across the ice. Sand? she wondered, and then the cardinal dropped gracefully out of the tree and started to peck at the ground. Of course, Jenny told herself—birdseed. The cardinal had just been waiting for breakfast to be served.

Then, across the yard, carefully picking her way, came a wide-eyed deer. Her long slim legs looked uncertain on the slick surfaces, and Jenny held her breath, waiting for the doe to fall. But she didn't, and she, too, found her way to the patch of ice, sniffed over the contents, and started to eat. The cardinal tipped his head warily and moved a little, but continued to consume his own meal.

'It's right out of Walt Disney,' Jenny mused. 'Thumper will turn up any minute!' So Dane hunted deer in the fall and fed them in the winter, hmm? There must have been corn in that bucket, too. No wonder, she thought again, that he was careful who was invited up here. Dane didn't like being vulnerable, and a person could learn too much about him just by seeing him in these surroundings.

Jenny's heart swelled, observing him as he stood

quietly beside the house watching the deer and the
birds. It was obviously not the first time this had happened; the animals seemed to accept his presence as
commonplace. But Dane was anything but commonplace, and Jenny felt a quiet warmth spread over her
as she looked at him. She loved him; she could accept
it now as she had not been able to last night. She
loved him just as he was, even if at times he schemed
and plotted against her.

Even that, she supposed, was understandable. She
had hurt him deeply that day five years ago when they
had first discovered the primitive bond between them.
She vaguely remembered now that she had even told
him that he wasn't good enough for her—for an Ashley. That was a remark guaranteed to cut the proud
Dane to the quick, and guaranteed to make him want
to prove differently. She supposed that was what he
was still trying to do—to prove himself her equal, or
her superior, by preventing her from having the bakery and the house. Jenny could understand that. She
was proud, herself.

With a little perspective, she could realise that he
had never hurt her father, had never set out to do so.
All the people who had told her that Dane would
never harm Richard had been right, and she had been
wrong. She had been trying so hard to deny her love
for him that she had been willing to believe anything.

'And just where does that get you, Jenny?' she
mocked. 'Talk about being vulnerable!'

'I thought you were going to fix breakfast.' Dane

set his load of wood down and draped his coat over a chair.

Jenny jumped, spilling her coffee, and turned. 'Oh—I was just admiring your view.'

'It is nice, isn't it? Before I built the cabin, I used to bring a sleeping bag out here in the summertime just so I could look down across that valley before I went to sleep.'

'I saw your little friend, the doe,' she told him.

'She's pretty, isn't she? She had her baby hidden back in the timber last spring.'

'But not hidden well enough, I see.' Jenny started to dig in the kitchen cabinets.

'She didn't seem to care. I could go right up to her.' Dane took a loaf of bread out. 'The ice is softening up. If the road crews get out soon, it'll break up before noon.'

'That's good, I'd hate to miss Alison's party tonight. I want to welcome the new year in right this year. Are you going?'

'Sure. Alison throws a good party.'

'Taking Suzanne?' Jenny tried to make the question casual.

'Of course.' He sounded surprised.

And he was surprised, Jenny thought. Naturally he was taking Suzanne; who else was there? 'Is French toast all right?' she asked.

'Sure. There's bacon somewhere in the refrigerator. Are you so anxious to get back to town?'

'Of course. Margaret will be worried about us.'

'Is that your only reason?'

'And Alison's party. I don't have a Suzanne to worry about me, you know.' She emerged from a cabinet with an opened package of cookies. 'How long have these things been here?'

Dane picked one up and tried to break it in two. 'Just about forever, it looks like.'

'Well, it suggests a new product line. We could let the cookies age and sell them for paving blocks.' Jenny dropped the package in the wastebasket. 'What does Suzanne think of you spending all your time up here?'

'Suzanne's got nothing to do with it.'

'She will have, though. And what is she going to think about me being here overnight?' Jenny admired her calm tone. She didn't look at him as she put a thick slice of french toast on the griddle.

'Depends on whether anyone tells her.'

'In Twin Rivers? You've got to be kidding. Probably everybody already knows it, and nobody in this town keeps a secret.'

Dane was looking through the contents of a drawer. 'Here's a pack of cards. I'll take you on at rummy after breakfast.'

'I'm serious, Dane. Will it cause trouble for you?'

She finally had got his full attention. His grey eyes roamed over her speculatively. 'I can't imagine you really being concerned, Red. The only other possibility is that you're hoping it will get me into trouble. Are you trying to compromise me?'

'I doubt it could be done. Here's your breakfast.'

He carried the plates to the table. 'It might be a lot of fun to compromise you. Let's see. If I go back and tell Steve—who's head over heels in love with you, by the way—that I am really sorry but it was impossible to resist you…'

'That's not funny, Dane.'

'I thought it was.' But he was quiet through the rest of the meal.

After the dishes were washed, Dane hung up his towel and said, 'Rummy?'

Jenny shrugged. 'Why not? It'll pass the time.'

The cards were scarcely dealt before he said, 'I think I just solved a problem for both of us.'

'Oh? You're calling in a helicopter?'

'Not that problem. You want the challenge of managing the bakery, right?'

Jenny eyed him warily. 'Yes, but…'

'And I want to get away from it, so I can finish my doctorate and get into research all the time instead of the eight hours a week I manage to fit in now.'

'Looks more like forty to me.'

He ignored her. 'But your father won't hear of you in the manager's job. If I leave, he'll probably promote Steve.'

'Are you joking?' she demanded.

'No. I know how Richard's mind works. Unless he was assured that I would back you up and support you…'

'Which you won't do.'

'I could be persuaded. I'll get to that. But right now I'm locked into the job. I already have a lot of financial responsibility, and now I've signed a mortgage too. So I can't just leave the job and live on a graduate assistant's pay.'

'Why not give up the mortgage?'

'Because I don't want to. I told you I like that house. I've always liked the idea of living there. When I was just a kid delivering newspapers on your block, I used to stand and stare at that house and wonder what it was like inside. And once in a while when it was cold Muriel would invite me into the kitchen and warm me up with hot chocolate and cookies. You were there once. You were about seven, and your hair was in pigtails, and you still had chubby cheeks...'

Jenny briskly sorted her cards. 'Are you going to play or talk? Do you want that discard?'

'No,' said Dane. 'I think I'll just keep what's been dealt into my hand.' The tone of his voice was solemn, and when Jenny looked up in surprise, she realised that he wasn't looking at the cards, but at her.

'And precisely what does that mean?'

He didn't answer, just tossed his cards down and leaned forward, arms braced on the table. 'You want the bakery, Jenny. I want to get out of it.'

'Don't insult my intelligence, Dane. You wouldn't leave that business, no matter what.'

'But I would, if I didn't have to give up the income. And that's where we can make a deal. Let's face it,

Jenny, if you stay here we're going to have to declare a truce sooner or later, out of exhaustion if nothing else. We can't go on in this unceasing war for ever.'

'I don't see why I should negotiate.'

'Out of respect for your father. It doesn't make it easy on him when we're quarrelling like two children in a sandpile. As long as you're here, you're going to be trying to get me fired, and if you ever should happen to succeed, I'll make your life so miserable hell would look pleasant by comparison.'

'You couldn't do it,' Jenny assured him.

'No? I'd still be a stockholder. Haven't you ever heard of stockholders who ask uncomfortable questions?'

Jenny shifted uneasily in her chair, and Dane grinned. 'All right,' she said. 'What do you propose as a solution?'

'Funny you should use that word,' he mused. 'I think we ought to get married.'

The cards slipped from Jenny's suddenly nerveless hand and fluttered to the floor. She bent to pick them up, and by the time she straightened, she had got her breath back. 'Don't be ridiculous!'

'It's not ridiculous; it's a perfectly reasonable solution to a problem we've found ourselves trapped in.' He reached for her hand. Jenny moved it out of his reach. 'You haven't studied the case on its merits, as I have.'

'What merit? Marriage?'

Dane sounded hurt. 'You don't need to say it as if it's an obscene word!'

'Under these circumstances, I think it is,' she said.

'Why? Business marriages occur in the best of families. Or call it an advantageous marriage, if you like.'

'Advantageous for whom?'

'For both of us. You get the bakery, I get my freedom to finish my doctorate, we both get a steady income, and we both get the house. Besides, Richard and Mother would be delighted.'

'Until they found out they had to announce it. I can hear it now—Mr Richard Ashley announces the engagement of his daughter Jennifer to Dane Sutherland, son of Mrs Richard Ashley. This is utterly ridiculous, Dane.'

'All right, then we'll stop talking about it.' He swept his cards up and rearranged them, played three aces, and discarded the jack of diamonds. Then his eyes narrowed on Jenny. 'Well?' he asked.

She picked up her cards. Her hands were shaking. A business deal. An advantageous marriage. It sounded like what Rosemary would say—or do. Jenny didn't want an advantageous marriage; she wanted to be in love.

But you are. The thought came so clearly that for an instant she thought she had said the words aloud. 'Why don't I just promise you fifty percent of the profits, and you can go do whatever it is you want to do?'

Dane put his cards down and ticked his points off

on his fingers. 'One—that leaves the house out of the deal, and you seem to be very angry about that. Two—it would be a problem to make it all legal. I'd much rather have community property law on my side. Three—with my luck, I'll be stuck there for another ten years and you'll convince him to will it to you, anyway. I want the whole show, not a minor third of it. Four—your father might still promote Steve, but if you're my wife, he won't. He can delude himself into thinking that I'm still controlling the strings. And five—if you're going to be difficult, I might as well stay where I am and bring in another assistant manager. I can always dabble in chemistry in my spare time. Enough?'

'It would also have the advantage of letting you marry Suzanne,' she pointed out.

'I'm not sure I consider marrying Suzanne an advantage. Where did you get the idea that I want to, anyway?'

'From Suzanne.'

'Be reasonable! Suzanne can't support me while I finish school.'

'It all comes back to money, doesn't it, Dane?' Jenny said coldly.

'Doesn't it always, darling?' He studied his cards. 'Think about it, Red. Let me know. Do you want the jack of diamonds, or are you going to draw?'

CHAPTER ELEVEN

THE PALE WINTER SUN was shining, and the weather had warmed slightly, just enough for the ice on the streets to be breaking up under the sand, salt and heavy traffic. But the sidewalks were still treacherous, and Jenny picked her way carefully down the hill to the lagoons. Much of the pond's surface had frozen, but in the protection of one of the high banks, a flock of ducks was swimming in water kept open only by their efforts. Jenny watched the furious paddling that it took to keep the frigid water from freezing, and took the first slice of bread out of the bag.

Is it enough? she asked herself as she flung the bits of bread to the ducks. Is it enough that I want Dane? Does it matter that he only wants me because of the bakery?

At least I know that from the start, she considered. He didn't lie to me.

He had been so quiet on the way back to town that she had wondered if he had regretted his proposal. The drive had been nerve-racking, of course, with the ice still treacherous, but even after they were on cleared roads Dane had been silent and distant. He was a different person up there in the woods—calmer, more at peace with himself.

She saw Finnegan coming down the hill and braced herself for the dog's enthusiastic greeting. The big setter reared up, his tongue lolling, ready to kiss her hello, and Jenny had to fend him off.

'Finnegan!' Dane ordered sharply, and the dog dropped to all fours, tail tucked, and slunk behind his master.

'Hi, Dane.' Jenny turned her attention back to the ducks.

'I thought you'd be getting ready for Alison's party, but Muriel said you'd come down here.'

Jenny glanced at her watch. 'Is it so late already?'

'Yes. The wrecker has even been out to get your car.'

'Is it all right?' she asked.

'Seems to be. But he's going to keep it for a couple of days and check it out. I don't want you driving it till I'm sure it's safe.'

The proprietorial note in his voice made Jenny bristle for a moment. He was right, she knew; after any kind of accident it made sense not to drive until the car had been inspected. Then she realised that if she married him, Dane would have every right to give those kind of orders. A sudden feeling of being warm and protected swept over her. So Dane did care about her after all; he'd given himself away. Perhaps it wasn't the way she would have chosen, but he did care. Was it enough to build a marriage on?

She flung another slice of bread to the ducks and handed one to Dane. 'Make yourself useful,' she ordered.

He obediently tore the slice into bitesized pieces and lobbed them one at a time into the water. 'You've had all day to think about it, Jenny,' he said after a moment. 'May I have my answer?'

She was silent for a few moments. This was a decision that would come only once, she knew. She must be very sure her answer was the right one. She stared out over the water, hands deep in the pockets of her jeans, and considered what she would say.

Her finger tips touched a stray coin, and she wondered idly what Dane would do if she pulled it out and flipped it. Heads I'll marry you, tails I won't, she thought. That ought to break through his calm.

Then her curiosity got the better of her. 'Don't you mind that just three days ago I was engaged to Brian?'

'Should I mind? I always considered Brian to be merely a game you were playing.' He reached for another slice of bread.

'I am on the rebound you know.'

'Perhaps you are. If we were declaring undying love, that would probably bother me. But I think we're going into this with our eyes open.'

'So you don't think it makes any difference.' She didn't look at him.

'No. I don't see how it can.'

'What about Suzanne? She thinks you're going to marry her.'

'Suzanne's a fool. I'll take care of her; you don't need to worry about her.'

Jenny hoped she wasn't there to see the scene. 'If I marry you, Dane, I don't want Daddy or Margaret or anyone to know why.'

'Arranged marriages for business reasons happen in the best of families, Jenny.'

'I don't want it to be public information.'

'You really care about that, don't you? All right. Anything else?'

'Yes. Ever since I was a little girl, I've dreamed of what my wedding would be like. I want a big church wedding, Dane. White gown and orange blossom and Daddy walking me down the aisle and Margaret crying into her lace handkerchief and somebody singing the 'Ave Maria'—I want all that. Besides, Margaret and Daddy will want it too.'

'All right.' His tone was casual and he reached for another slice of bread.

'Dane, I will not be married out in the woods by a justice of the peace with Finnegan as your best man!'

'Nobody's asking you to, Jenny. I agreed, and I meant it.'

'But you didn't even think about it. You don't know what you're agreeing to. You'll have to wear a tuxedo.'

'As long as it's not a white one, I think I'll survive the experience.'

Jenny was not amused. 'You have to promise about the necktie.'

He held up a hand. 'Scout's honour, I will wear a tie on my wedding day. Anything else I should know about?'

'I think that takes care of it.'

'Then shall we seal the contract with a kiss?'

'Wouldn't a handshake be more appropriate? And I haven't said I'd marry you yet.'

'Yes, you have. All the rest was minor detail.' His hands were firm on her shoulders as he drew her close.

DANE WAS ALREADY at the party when Jenny arrived with Steve. Unusual, to be attending the first party of her engagement with a man she wasn't engaged to, she thought. But they had decided to wait till New Year's Day to make their announcement.

As soon as Jenny came into Alison's living room she saw Dane across the room, glass in hand and Suzanne hanging on his arm. It looked as if he was going to take advantage of the last night of his freedom. And Jenny remembered what he had told Dr Grantham on Christmas Day—something about the lucky man being the one who didn't get the girl.

She drifted through the party in a daze, scarcely noticing Steve at her elbow, scarcely hearing the noise and hilarity of the group. She saw only Dane smiling down at Suzanne, heard only Dane's laughter.

You're jealous, Jenny, she told herself crossly. And you'd better get over it. Dane is Dane, and nothing will ever change him; you agreed to take what he offered and now you're upset because it isn't more.

She escaped from the crowd and slipped down the darkened hallway to the nursery where Molly slept, undisturbed by the party. Jenny hung over the crib, watching the baby breathe and marvelling that anything so tiny could be so perfectly formed. One small hand had escaped from under the blanket and was half-curled next to Molly's mouth as if she was thinking about sucking her thumb. Jenny tucked it back under the blanket. Molly sighed, turned her dark-fuzzed head, and pulled her knees up under her stomach.

Maybe next year, Jenny thought, there will be a nursery in my house. And I can watch my own baby sleep, a little boy with dark hair and grey eyes who will grow to be as tall as Dane...

Just last weekend she had been engaged to Brian and confidently planning to mother his children. But would she have gone through with it? Probably not, Jenny decided. If Brian had offered her that ring at a less sentimental and public time, she might have simply refused it. Even if she had worn it, with an engagement at least six months long, they would never have made it to the altar. Brian had been just a game she was playing; Dane was right about that, even though he didn't suspect why. All along Jenny had known, deep inside, that the only man for her was Dane.

But what if she wasn't the only woman for him?

The question rang inside her with the tiredness of repetition as she tucked Molly's hand under the blanket again and gently closed the nursery door behind her.

The chatter and rumble of the party going on down the hall reached her ears, and Jenny leaned against the door, not wanting to go back there, yet not knowing what else to do.

And then she saw them.

They were standing at the end of the darkened hall, as far as possible from the party, and they were locked in each other's arms. Dane's back was to her, but Jenny could see Suzanne's blonde hair cascading over his arm, and the girl's arms were tight around him.

He must have just told her, Jenny thought calmly, and this is her answer. This is her despair. And was Dane despairing too, she wondered, or was he glad to be rid of Suzanne?

She saw it clearly, all of a sudden. Of course he was glad to be rid of Suzanne; she was entertaining, but that was not enough to hold Dane. There would, however, always be someone.

Jenny wondered how many other Suzannes there would be through the years. How many times would she have to watch this and pretend when he came home to her that it hadn't happened? Because, after all, as long as she had his name and the bakery, she had no right to anything else. That had been the agreement.

Quietly, Jenny found her coat in the hall closet, slipped through the kitchen and out the back door, and started up the hill towards home. It was an hour till midnight. If she was lucky, no one would miss her till then.

The house was quiet and dark. Lucifer came to meet her at the door, stropping himself against her ankles. She picked him up and tiptoed through the big living room and up the stairs, happy that her father and Margaret had decided on an early night. She knew she couldn't face them tonight.

Her room was warm and silent except for Lucifer purring in her arms, but the comfort she sought was not there. She leaned against the door and remembered the night Dane had been in her room, the way he had lounged on her bed and teased her, the ferocious gentleness of his kisses, the hunger that had wakened inside her. Why had she not known then? she wondered. How could she have been so blind? All the man had to do was look at her and she forgot everything except her need of him. It certainly wasn't Jenny who had kept them out of bed.

And it would happen again. He would have his other women, and he would come home to Jenny, and she would melt because she loved him. Could she endure the kind of torment it would be every time she saw him with another woman? Suzanne was past, but there would be other Suzannes. None of them could hold him long, but neither could Jenny. Only the bakery could hold him.

She had to get away, she realised suddenly. She had to think about it, to decide whether she could live with the knowledge that she would never be the only woman in his life—that she wouldn't be in his life at all if she wasn't Richard Ashley's daughter.

She laughed suddenly, a laugh totally without humour. The instant she had realised Brian wanted to marry Rosemary's daughter she had wanted nothing more to do with him. But with Dane it was different.

She emptied drawers in a frenzy, throwing clothes into her bags without a care for how they landed. Tears swam in her enormous brown eyes. Damn him, she thought viciously. He could have allowed me my dreams. He didn't have to show me on the first night of our engagement just how little it meant to him. He didn't have to stand there in Alison's house and kiss Suzanne as if his world was ending. But he had.

Just hours ago she had been so sure that she could marry him, and live with him, and love him despite his lack of love for her. He cared a little for her. And she wanted him every bit as much as he wanted her. It had been enough—then.

She angrily mopped tears off her cheeks with the back of her hand. 'That lousy, lowdown son of a...' Her voice broke on a sob, and she stood with her hands braced on the opened drawer, fighting for control.

'Go on, Jenny. I'm sure there's more you'd like to say about me.'

She whirled to see Dane leaning against the door, arms folded across his chest. 'Get out of here!' she ordered.

He ignored her. 'Where are you going?'

'Home.' She pulled open another drawer.

'You told me this afternoon that you'd stay and make this our home.'

'I've obviously changed my mind, wouldn't you say?'

'Then we'll just have to change it back.' He pushed himself away from the door and started across the room.

Jenny backed away. 'No, Dane!' She was improvising wildly, grasping at the chaotic thoughts that swirled through her mind. 'I wanted the bakery, and I thought I could overcome the revulsion I feel when you touch me... But I can't.'

He smiled and lifted a hand to brush a red curl back from her tear-stained cheek.

'Then why the tears, my dear? You're a dreadful liar, Jenny.'

She shivered.

'So you're revolted when I touch you?' he mused.

'Yes!' She tried to run, but she had backed into the armchair by the window, and Dane, towering over her, could easily block her escape.

'Let's prove it, shall we? You didn't seem revolted this morning up at the cabin. When I came in to wake you, you curled up against me like Lucifer does—a fierce little kitten who's hungry for love. Perhaps I should have made love to you as you've been begging me to do.'

'I've never begged for anything. Certainly not that!'

'You don't have to use words to beg, my dear.' In one fluid movement he had picked her up and tossed her on to the four-poster bed. She scrambled for the edge, but in an instant he was beside her, his hands warm and firm as he held her there.

Jenny looked up into his eyes. One last kiss, she thought. Surely she could have that to remember. Then sanity returned. One last kiss would lead to nothing but trouble. One last kiss and every resolve would melt. Better to be without him, to bear the pain of being alone, than to have him only part of the time, and know that some other woman was consoling him.

'No matter what methods you use, Dane, I am not going to marry you,' she said. The tone of her voice was deadly calm.

It stopped him cold, as nothing else could have. He left her there and slowly crossed the room to stare out of the window. 'Why not, Jenny?' he asked at last, his voice husky. 'Because I'm not good enough for you—for an Ashley?' Under the sarcastic words lay raw pain. Five-year-old pain, she realised, with a stab of recognition.

'No, Dane.' Her voice was quiet. 'I hope I've grown up that much.'

'Then why?' he demanded.

'Leave it alone. You can have my stock in the bakery; I don't want anything to do with it.'

'I'll take it. Fifty a share, I think we've said?'

She was stunned. She had expected him to brush the offer aside. 'Is that all that matters to you, Dane?'

'No. But I want that stock. And I also want to know why you changed your mind.'

Jenny straightened the spread on the bed, willing her hands not to tremble. 'I don't think it's necessary to go into details.'

'That's where you're wrong, Red. I want every detail, and I'll get it if I have to shake it out of you!'

Looking at him, she didn't doubt it. He looked quite capable of murder. 'Why? You have what you wanted.'

'Who makes you the expert on what I want?' He was advancing on her, his face grim.

Jenny's control snapped. What difference did it make, anyway? she thought. Let him have the pound of flesh he demanded. She'd never see him again; what difference did it make if he knew the truth?

'Oh, you've got your revenge, Dane,' she said, and her voice shook. 'So gloat all you want. I saw you with Suzanne—you meant me to see, didn't you? I won't marry you because it would kill me to be your wife and know you still have your other women out there.'

'Say it, Jenny. I have to hear it all.'

'My God, you ask a high price! I fell in love with you! Is that what you wanted me to say? Well, it's true. You can put that under your pillow every night.'

'I will,' he said quietly.

The silence was a cloud between them. Then Dane

said, 'I've waited five years for you to say that, Jenny. I never thought you would. I tried to forget you. I thought I was getting over you. Then when you came back...' he shrugged, 'it was even worse.'

Jenny was stunned. 'You wanted me to leave!'

'Of course I did. It was too painful to have you here.' He smiled ruefully. 'But I knew your stubbornness would make you stay, if I told you to go. And even if it was painful to see you, it would have been worse to be without you again.'

'And I'm supposed to believe that you've pined for me?'

'Ask your father. I told him five years ago that I wanted to marry you.'

'To get the bakery. There's nothing new in that.'

'No, not for the bakery. Will you ever believe that I don't give a damn about the bakery?'

She dashed tears out of her eyes. 'Then why did you want to buy my stock?'

'Just to prove to you that it doesn't matter. You no longer own a single share, Jenny. And I still want to marry you.'

'Why?'

His smile was twisted. 'A good psychiatrist would probably tell me I like pain. You're a strange woman, my darling. You have no curiosity.'

Jenny sat down, head in her hands. Her mind was whirling. 'So what does that mean?'

'Any ordinary woman in your shoes would have been asking questions about the source of my income within fifteen minutes of landing in town. You don't really think I acquired the funds to buy that stock of yours by embezzling it from petty cash, do you?'

'Daddy pays you well.'

'He certainly does. But not that well. I don't live on a shoestring, Jenny—or hadn't you noticed?'

A picture of that snug little house up in the woods flashed into her mind. No corners cut, no luxuries left out, no expense spared... She had assumed that the bakery had built it. 'If it doesn't come from the bakery, then where are you getting all the money?'

'From Mother's perfume that you like so well. One of the big companies is test-marketing it right now. And from the new fresh scent they're now putting in fabric softener. And from...'

'From your lab,' Jenny breathed.

'You may go to the head of the class. I told you I wanted to be a full-time chemist. You thought it was an excuse to retire before I was thirty.'

She walked across the room and stared out over the twinkling lights, bounced back by the snow. Jim and Alison had tried to tell her about Dane's lab. But she hadn't been listening. 'I've reconsidered. I don't want to sell my stock.' Then she held her breath.

'Tell you what—I'll give it back to you as a wedding gift.'

'Dane...' She turned to face him. 'Can I believe you?'

'What would you like me to offer as proof? If my chequebook will do, it's right here. If you want a statement of my net worth, you'll have to wait till my accountant is back in his office after the holiday.'

Jenny was shaking her head. 'Oh, not the money—that's not important.' She sat down in the armchair and nibbled on a thumbnail.

'It has certainly seemed important to you for the last three weeks,' Dane murmured. 'Do you mean, why do I want to marry you?'

Jenny nodded. She felt like a fool as she dashed tears out of her eyes. What could he say, after all, that would convince her?

He sat down on the arm of her chair. 'Jenny,' he said gently, and stroked her hair, 'when you were fifteen, your first boy-friend found another girl. Remember?'

'Of course I remember. I thought I was going to die because he'd jilted me. So what?'

'You cried it all out in my arms. I was ready to kill him, and then I realised why. He'd had the nerve to hurt the girl I loved.'

'Did you really?'

'Love you? My God, yes. And you were so young. There wasn't one thing I could do about it. I couldn't even talk to your father, then—he'd have killed me.'

'You said you told him.'

'I did, later; that day that we've both been pretending wasn't important—when you were seventeen and I was going back to school. I told him what had happened and that I wanted to marry you.'

'What did he say?' Jenny's voice was rapt.

'He told me I was crazy, and that I had to give you a chance to grow up.' He laughed ruefully. 'You can't imagine how hard it was to stay away that spring, knowing you were dating all those boys. And then when I came home, you were gone.'

She put her head down on his shoulder. It seemed to belong there. 'I was scared of you,' she confessed. 'And of what I'd do when I saw you again.'

'I didn't think it was just a disagreement with your father,' Dane said softly. 'But I was afraid to let myself believe that I was important enough to make you do that.' He pulled her out of her chair and into his arms. 'These last few years haven't been easy, Jenny.'

'It hasn't exactly been comforting to see you with Suzanne, either,' Jenny retorted.

'Jealous? I'm glad.'

'You were kissing Suzanne tonight,' she pointed out.

'No, Suzanne was kissing me. There's a difference, though I am a little ashamed of myself for using her to make you angry. You've never had any competition, you know.' He ran a gentle finger down her cheek, scooping up the last tear. 'Do you think the bakery can handle the challenge of a ten-tiered wedding cake with a champagne fountain?'

She smiled mistily up at him. 'I'll get married in the woods if you want to.'

'Absolutely not. This is going to be the biggest splash Twin Rivers has ever seen. No small private ceremony or anything like that—we aren't giving anyone the opportunity to make snide remarks.'

Jenny shivered a little with happiness.

'When did you realise it?' he demanded, pulling her even closer. 'That you love me?'

'Last night. Pretty slow, wasn't I?'

'Dreadfully. When are you going to marry me?' But he was kissing her before she had a chance to reply.

The world is a delightful place, Jenny thought dreamily, giving herself up to the pleasure of his embrace. Her fingers tangled themselves in his hair. 'June is a nice month,' she murmured.

'So's January. Shall we compromise on it?'

'I need some time to get things ready, Dane. It does take a while to design a ten-tiered cake, after all. What about May?'

'What about no later than the middle of February? I've waited five years, Jenny. Don't make me suffer any more.'

'All right,' Jenny said demurely. 'I won't.'

Down in the living room the grandfather clock chimed midnight, but neither of them was interested in welcoming a new year.

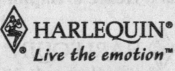

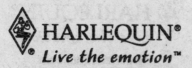

…there's more to the story!

Superromance.
A *big* satisfying read about unforgettable
characters. Each month we offer *six* very different
stories that range from family drama to adventure
and mystery, from highly emotional stories to
romantic comedies—and much more! Stories
about people you'll believe in and care about.
Stories too compelling to put down….

Our authors are among today's *best* romance
writers. You'll find familiar names and talented
newcomers. Many of them are award winners—
and you'll see why!

If you want the biggest and best
in romance fiction, you'll get it
from Superromance!

Emotional, Exciting, Unexpected…

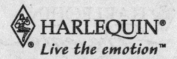

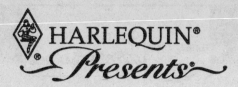

HARLEQUIN®
Presents

The world's bestselling romance series...
The series that brings you your favorite authors,
month after month:

Helen Bianchin...Emma Darcy
Lynne Graham...Penny Jordan
Miranda Lee...Sandra Marton
Anne Mather...Carole Mortimer
Susan Napier...Michelle Reid

and many more uniquely talented authors!

Wealthy, powerful, gorgeous men...
Women who have feelings just like your own...
The stories you love, set in exotic, glamorous locations...

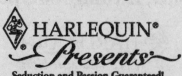

HARLEQUIN®
Presents

Seduction and Passion Guaranteed!

HPDIR104

Harlequin Historicals®
Historical Romantic Adventure!

From rugged lawmen and valiant knights to defiant heiresses and spirited frontierswomen, Harlequin Historicals will capture your imagination with their dramatic scope, passion and adventure.

Harlequin Historicals . . . they're too good to miss!

HARLEQUIN®
INTRIGUE®
WE'LL LEAVE YOU BREATHLESS!

If you've been looking for thrilling tales of
contemporary passion and sensuous love stories
with taut, edge-of-the-seat suspense—then
you'll love Harlequin Intrigue!

Every month, you'll meet six new heroes
who are guaranteed to make your spine tingle
and your pulse pound. With them you'll enter
into the exciting world of Harlequin Intrigue—
where your life is on the line
and so is your heart!

THAT'S INTRIGUE—
ROMANTIC SUSPENSE
AT ITS BEST!

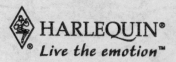

HARLEQUIN®
Live the emotion™

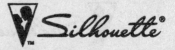

passionate powerful provocative love stories

**Silhouette Desire delivers
strong heroes, spirited heroines
and compelling love stories.**

Desire features your favorite authors,
including

Annette Broadrick,
Ann Major,
Anne McAllister
and Cait London.

**Passionate, powerful and provocative
romances *guaranteed!***

For superlative authors, sensual stories
and sexy heroes, choose Silhouette Desire.

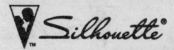

passionate powerful provocative love stories